SHOTGUNNER

Wes Garrick, the Blayrock freighter, was known for the expert handling of his repeating shotgun if things got rough. When a friend, rancher Jim Farrer, was falsely accused by the men from C Star and had to go on the run, Garrick felt he should take a hand. He was soon in confrontation with those who were determined to see Farrer nailed as a rustler. Gunmen were brought in, and Garrick himself became the quarry in a deadly game of stalk-and-kill.

Books by Lee F. Gregson
in the Linford Western Library:

THE MAN OUT THERE
THE STOREKEEPER OF SLEEMAN
LONG AGO IN SERAFINA
SEASON OF DEATH
BRAID
THE DEATH MAN
HAUCK RIVER GUNS

LEE F. GREGSON

SHOTGUNNER

Complete and Unabridged

LINFORD
Leicester

First published in Great Britain in 1994 by
Robert Hale Limited
London

First Linford Edition
published 1999
by arrangement with
Robert Hale Limited
London

The moral right of the author has been asserted

British Library CIP Data

Gregson, Lee F.
    Shotgunner.—Large print ed.—
    Linford western library
    1. Large type books
    2. Western stories
    I. Title
    823.9'14 [F]

    ISBN 0–7089–5571–1

Published by
F. A. Thorpe (Publishing) Ltd.
Anstey, Leicestershire

Set by Words & Graphics Ltd.
Anstey, Leicestershire
Printed and bound in Great Britain by
T. J. International Ltd., Padstow, Cornwall

This book is printed on acid-free paper

1

On a dusty, well-defined trail winding through cattle country, two freight wagons, each drawn by a six-horse team, and their cargoes covered by lashed-down green tarpaulins, were now some five miles short of the town of Blayrock, the haze of which could now faintly be discerned in the heat-shimmering distance. Being purposely held back to avoid the worst of the white dust, the second wagon was trailing the other by almost a hundred yards.

The drivers of both wagons, however, had noticed the appearance some little distance away to their right of a small group of riders, quite clearly angling towards them, and though this was familiar territory to both the freighters, the man on the seat of the lead-wagon reached back under the tarpaulin behind him and with one hand drew better within his reach the loaded shotgun that he always kept there. A 10-gauge with a rolled-steel, full-choke barrel, it was a repeater model, lever action, with four cartridges in a tubular magazine beneath the barrel, as well as the one in the chamber, the butt of plain wood with a butt-plate of hard rubber. The gun weighed about eight pounds and when fired produced a kick like a bad-tempered *burro*; but in the hands of a competent shotgunner, anywhere at short range it was a highly dangerous weapon. Garrick's freight line seldom carried what might be thought of as valuables; it was just that sometimes, in this raw country, a man needed to reinforce his intentions with something more positive than words. The sight of the repeating shotgun was quite positive enough for the tastes of most people. The two wagons went on their creaking way, harness jingling and clinking, the drivers seemingly concentrating solely upon the trail that lay ahead of them.

Within a very few minutes the group of horsemen had been revealed as three in number, all dressed in the manner of range men, and quite soon were identifiable as a rancher of those parts, Clayburgh of C Star, his foreman, a man named Dehl, and a rider called Hagan.

On the lead-wagon Garrick hauled back on his long ribbons, and calling, brought his team down to a halt, dust rising all around the heavy rig, and after he had stopped he could hear the sounds of the following wagon, Elder's, continuing to come, closing the distance until finally it was pulled to a stop to the left of Garrick's wagon and almost level with it.

'Dan Clayburgh,' Elder said. His lined face under his wide brimmed hat was sweat-runnelled through a plaster of alkali dust and his old green shirt had large sweat patches all over it.

Garrick nodded, his attention on the three riders coming in, sensing an urgent purpose about them that was not quite natural. Garrick was a tall, strongly built man in his mid-thirties, wearing denims and a battered dark grey hat with a shallow crown, his skin deeply tanned and a good deal ravaged by the sun, the hair bunching at his neck very dark, as dark as the eyes, now narrowed, fastened on Clayburgh and his men as they trotted in the final thirty yards and drew to a halt near Garrick's wagon.

Greetings were perfunctory. For some reason Clayburgh was clearly in no humour for small-talk. His horse and those of Dehl and Hagan was sweat-rimed and dusty and the riders were scarcely in better condition. Clayburgh was a burly, leather-faced man of perhaps fifty, who had run C Star since his mid-twenties, after the death of his father, developing the spread until it had become one of the bigger and more prosperous in the territory. A blunt, uncompromising individual, Clayburgh was also a man of uncertain temper, a man to be avoided if he felt that matters which ought to be going his way, were not. Now he wasted no time.

'Yuh come direct from Benning Forks, Garrick?'

Garrick nodded, pushed his hat back off his forehead. 'Yeah, we have. Why?' He allowed his unflurried gaze to go from Clayburgh to the ox-like Dehl, to Hagan's pinched, freckled face and back to Clayburgh.

'I'm about ready to stretch necks is why,' Clayburgh said, 'an' before too much longer, believe me, I'll do just that.' So that was it. He scarcely needed to elaborate. For some time past, Clayburgh had been complaining bitterly about losses of stock, insisting that small numbers were being run off, but regularly and over a long period, and that in total, his losses must amount to more than four hundred head. He had not been reticent about his suspicions, either, having had his hard eyes on first one, then another, and frequently had gone looking over a broad area and had made widespread enquiries and issued dire threats, but to no result. 'Near to fifty head gone now,' he said, 'that I know was in a canyon sou' west o' Blayrock, an' I tell yuh, Garrick, I've plain had enough. So what I want to know from yuh is if you seen anybody, anybody at all 'twixt here an' Benning Forks; people known, strangers, anybody on the move. It might sound like the wrong direction but I got to look all over. All over.'

'We saw nobody,' said Garrick, 'except Bolt, on his own, in the Forks, an' we came up with him again on his way back to Diamond B. Just Nate.'

Dehl's hard voice grunted, 'Bolt. Christ, was the bastard sober?'

'Just,' said Garrick.

Clayburgh lifted his sweat-stained hat off and with a forearm, wiped his forehead and replaced the hat. Bolt, Garrick was well aware, had been at certain times in the past, a man, among others, whom Clayburgh had had his eye on over theft of stock. This time, however, his interest seemed to wane

6

quickly as far as Bolt was concerned, and Garrick came to the conclusion that Clayburgh, having no doubt failed to find and follow any trail that there might have been in some more likely area, was now casting about more randomly, in anger and frustration, in the vague hope of turning up information from less likely sources and in quite unlikely places. Then he looked at Garrick keenly.

'Might be I'll have me a word or two with Bolt, anyway; then maybe another one or two with that great friend o' yours, Mister Jim Farrer.'

If it was designed to unsettle Garrick it did not have any visible effect, Garrick merely regarding the rancher narrowly but calmly, ignoring too the bold stares of Dehl and Hagan, and knowing that Elder's eyes would also be fastened on him. Dehl's horse tossing its head, had half turned, putting it nearer to the wagon, and Garrick knew also that the C Star foreman's eyes had noticed the big shotgun lying behind the driver; but that would not have come as any surprise to Dehl, for Garrick's familiarity with the weapon, his preference for it, was widely known.

Garrick, still looking at Clayburgh, said evenly:

'Then I sure do wish you luck, Dan. If you do go lookin' for your cows on Jim Farrer's range, if I was you I'd kind of whisper when you ask him about 'em.'

'Farrer don't cut no ice at all.' This was Dehl butting in, his broad, brutish, dusty face sweating profusely, a droplet gathered on his round chin. Dehl, it was said, had spent much time over many months combing hills and canyons, riding far and wide, seeking signs of missing C Star cattle.

Garrick looked at Dehl. 'Just the same, Dave, I'd take special care, real special care, was I you.'

'Nobody on C Star needs any o' your advice,' Dehl said, and when Hagan, too, looked to be about ready to shove

8

an oar in, Clayburgh glanced sharply at them.

'Leave it.' To Garrick he then said, 'Yuh see anything, partic'ly any strangers, I'd be obliged to hear word.' Garrick knew that he was simply reviving old talk, talk reaching back more than a year around Blayrock and the surrounding ranches, riders seen moving on the foothills of the Chaters, riders no one had yet identified. From time to time, of course, strangers were to be seen passing through Blayrock itself, and all of these were considered by Clayburgh when he got to hear about them, as deeply suspicious. But in Blayrock, as elsewhere, it was not the custom and indeed was not at all wise to question a man simply because he was not known thereabouts. Whoever he was, as long as he perceivably broke no law, what any individual did or what his business might be, must remain strictly his own affair; and although, more than once, Clayburgh had seen fit to take it up with the Blayrock peace officer,

Wenlake, in an effort to persuade him to make enquiries, he had got nowhere and indeed, probably had not expected to.

Garrick nodded but did not himself comment one way or another. He looked around at the silent, patient Elder on the other wagon and nodded to him as well, and as one, and without another glance at the C Star men, they whistled and took up their long whips and got their groaning rigs on the move again.

For a short distance the two big freight wagons moved along together as both Garrick and his driver, Elder, watched the three men from the C Star riding away. After a few minutes, Elder called:

'Must've meant what he said, Wes.'

Garrick had come to the same conclusion. If Clayburgh persisted with his present line of ride, he must inevitably, and soon, pass onto range belonging to the Flying F, to Jim Farrer. A strange uneasiness began stirring in

Garrick as he went driving on, for he knew that Farrer was not a man given to wilting under pressure or taking kindly to aggression such as he might be faced with from his neighbour, and in particular from Dave Dehl. On the contrary, Farrer could be a tough, quick-tempered and even stubborn man if he thought he was being pushed, and Garrick considered that, in present circumstances, this might well lead to a confrontation, for Clayburgh, by the looks of him, was truly incensed, and this time there would be little diplomacy to be expected from him in his dealings with Farrer or anybody else. Garrick called sharply to his team, cracked the long whip and gradually drew ahead and away from Elder's wagon, freshly anxious to get the freight into Blayrock, looking forward to seeing Emily once again, yet disturbed enough by now to consider perhaps paying a visit to Jim and Liz Farrer. Freight which needed to be taken on to places beyond Blayrock could be hauled by Elder in one wagon.

The sharp angles of the town's buildings were now plain to see as was the haze of chimney smoke which, even in the warmest of weather, seemed always to hang over it. Beyond Blayrock, across these rolling range-lands, lay the loaf-like foothills and then the dark slits of canyons rising to the heat-misted jaggedness of the Chater Range that ran away into farther distance. Of the towns that lay beyond Blayrock, Georgeville, Bannock, Miner's River, none were yet linked by railroad, so that all journeys in this region were by horse or by stage, all freight still hauled by outfits such as Garrick's, feeding in from larger towns lying to the north-east, places like Benning Forks. So there was a certain sense of isolation about Blayrock, surrounded by cattle outfits, and it was this which sometimes troubled Garrick, knowing the problems faced sometimes by Emily's father, George Wenlake, in his efforts to maintain the peace against the presence of people such as Clayburgh and his often troublesome foreman, Dave Dehl; and a few miles in another direction, but often in Blayrock, the owner of the run-down Diamond B, Nathan Bolt, with his legendary propensity for the bottle. People like Jim and Liz Farrer, trying to live their own lives, conduct their own affairs in peace, tended to balance matters somewhat. But this time Garrick had been jolted by the obvious, unswerving purpose of Clayburgh, and sensed that once the acrimony came to the surface, perhaps with outright accusations starting to fly, matters might so very easily turn ugly. And though he continually tried, for the sake of his own freight business, to keep his peace with all factions in any dispute, some were inclined to see him as aligned with Wenlake because of his closeness to Emily Wenlake; and at the same time it was universally known that his most trusted friend was the rancher, Farrer. As he now came nearer to Blayrock, some sixth sense left him with an emptiness behind his belt buckle, a premonition, perhaps, of violent change to come.

2

The hammering noises were of Smith the hired hand carrying out repairs to one of the doors of the loft above the barn, one of his boots planted out on the hoist beam above the yard. The clattering sounds were from Liz Farrer clearing away breakfast dishes as Farrer himself prepared to depart; but when he said he would be out along the south-west line and would not be back until later in the day, she did not answer him. He walked out on the back porch, settling his hat on his head. Farrer clumped on down the steps and went across the already warm yard towards the barn. Clearly it was to be another time of strain, not much said, Liz not wanting to engage his eye, Farrer himself feeling easier in his mind when he was out of the house and away. It was just one more weight to be added to the burden of his days, another problem waiting for solution among the accumulating problems on the Flying F.

Money was becoming even scarcer, costs rising, beef prices unremarkable, and Farrer believed that he was now caught in a game that was no longer winnable. Soon he might have to dispense with Smith's services. What he needed most was one, or even better, two hold-off seasons in which to build up his herd, during which time prices might well improve and bring him back into a stronger financial position from which he could develop; and at the same time retire debt. But there was no hold-off period among those who loaned funds. Year by year he needed to turn beef into whatever money he could get for it, and raising further loans was now out of the question. And with less than enough money flowing through the outfit he had had problems in hiring enough help at roundup and the hands that he had hired on had not always been of the kind that he had wanted.

Even so, with Liz to back him and give him encouragement he had always retained the will to battle on through difficult times, and so far they had overcome all sorts of obstacles and survived setbacks through the vagaries of climate and the ravages of predators of one sort or another.

As he rode away now, however, it was as much to be with himself, to gather his private thoughts, as for any other purpose, though it was his intention to ride up into the foothills of the Chaters to see if he could find any signs of travellers having been on his range during recent times. Smith had felt quite sure he had seen riders well inside the Flying F line and though, ordinarily, that might have caused him small concern, when he had made as though to get closer to them they had at once ridden away and passed rapidly from sight. Smith, however, had caught a metallic glint and had been of the opinion that whoever they were they had had a glass on him. Ever mindful of

Clayburgh's long-standing complaints of rustling, Farrer now thought that he ought at least to go on up there and take a look around, for Clayburgh aside, he himself could not afford to lose any stock. And now there was this other thing, with Liz. No outright disagreements; not yet anyway, but real close to it once or twice. No, not rows, but unaccustomed silences, a drawing apart, a resentment, almost; a barrier that he had seemed unable to breach.

In a little more than a couple of hours he was urging the big chestnut in among the dry hills, and within an hour after that, there lay before him the riven rock of the lower Chaters, the dark slits of canyons cutting the sun-hot faces of the mountains towering away above him. On the way in here he had noticed pockets of a few head of cattle with his own brand on them, animals that ought to be choused out onto the range proper, but that was not his purpose today. Relying on what Smith had said to him, Farrer had made his approach

18

so that he would be in the general area in which the ranch hand claimed to have seen the unknown riders.

Farrer made a search of the hill-slopes and the summit-line for a good half-hour until, hot and sweating, needing to take a long draught from his canteen, he came to the belief that either Smith had been mistaken or that he, Farrer, thinking of other matters, had misunderstood the direction he had been given. Then he noticed that, perhaps a half-mile away, buzzards were floating down to something among the rough, rocky feet of the Chaters. For several minutes Farrer watched, then turned the chestnut and headed in that direction looking for some way that would take him down and in among the crags. Once or twice, however, he was assailed by a feeling that he was being observed, but though he drew the horse to a halt and took a careful look around him, he was unable to discern the merest flicker of movement anywhere. By and by he saw that by going down a particular slope he would arrive in a sandy area of boulder-strewn ground through which he could pick his way and eventually come close to the place where he had seen the buzzards descending; so he urged the horse down the slope, casting one more glance around him as he went, but again seeing no evidence of any other presence.

On the sandy bottom, weaving in and out between reddish upthrusts of rock, the heights rearing above him, he went on in the enclosed, baking atmosphere for what he began to think was surely a longer distance than the half-mile he had estimated; then he passed between two great shoulders of rock and saw, running away on either hand, a narrow — perhaps thirty yards wide — sandy corridor that he now recalled having come upon in the past, but that he had seldom had need to venture into even when searching for strays, for it was by no means an easy place for man or beast and there was no natural feed; a place of ancient, probably volcanic rocks and little else.

Yet cattle had been here, cattle and horses both, for the passage of them was plain enough to see, and here and there were piles of fly-crawling dung; numbers of cattle and at least two horses, and whoever it was that had driven the beasts along this secluded way must have done so without haste and with not a little patience. Driven them from where and to where? Farrer brought the chestnut to a stop, the heat beating down on him in this windless place, flies buzzing around man and animal. Staring down at the undisturbed tracks he saw that by moving to his left he would be heading in the same direction as had this unknown herd. Moving off, eyes probing the dark rock-clefts, he was astonished when, ahead of him, the trail turned off to his right, where the wall of rock rose dizzily towards the delft blue of the sky, and it was a moment before he was able to comprehend that the shadows he was looking at were in fact not merely shadows but represented a fissure some forty-five feet in width, leading he knew not where, and was probably one of any number of such passageways to be found along the lower reaches of the Chaters, one scarcely distinguishable from another. True, while all of these would be considered to be a part of the Flying F, most would have remained virtually unvisited.

Farrer nudged the horse, moving into this shadowed place, still in soft footing, the rocky aperture widening on either side of him as he went, and as he so progressed, the sounds began coming to him; the quite unmistakable bawling of cattle, but sounds that were oddly distorted among the great rock faces. Now he rode slowly out into a lighter, wider place, until there, stretching before him was a high, blind canyon; and there they were, the cattle, standing in groups in this place where no feed existed and where there was no indication of water. Buzzards rose up, screeching, from the carcass of a dead cow. Farrer stopped the horse and it stood tossing its head, nostrils flaring at the smell of death. Farrer rubbed a gloved hand along its neck, soothing the animal, talking to it, then ran his eye over what he had discovered, figuring that there were better than two hundred head, some of them looking the worse for wear, but the bulk of them in good condition, suggesting that these had not been here for long. He kneed the now reluctant chestnut, walking it closer. He looked at one brand, another, then another, stopped the horse again, pushed his hat back from his sweat-runnelled forehead. The brands were C Star, these and as many others as he could discern, all C Star. And here they were on a part of the Flying F range, having been brought here by God-knew who, but clearly hidden away against — what? Against being moved on, he must assume, as the opportunity arose. Clayburgh had been right all along; Farrer felt both disturbed and angry; now, the distant riders Smith claimed to have seen made all kinds of sense.

Slowly Farrer turned his horse around. Alone, there was nothing more that he could do, so he would go on back to the ranch and send Smith away to fetch a C Star crew, then help them get these cattle out and back onto Clayburgh's range; and whatever Clayburgh chose to do after that would be entirely his affair. Farrer was curious to learn, however, exactly how they had got them in here without being seen. If they had moved them by night, as he would have expected, then they would have had to have scouted the terrain most carefully; then they would have had to fetch them perhaps out of draws and difficult places on Clayburgh's range, across part of the Flying F, in the open, then get them out of sight as soon as possible. So Farrer followed the trail along the soft going outside the canyon until eventually he passed into a short valley between dry hills and came at last out onto his own rolling and more familiar range, the shimmering distance stretching away before him.

★　★　★

It was sufficient to divert Liz, at least temporarily, from whatever it was that was troubling her.

'*Clayburgh*'s cows?'

'Yeah, I'd say all of 'em are. And they hadn't got in there without help.' He sighed. 'Where's Smith?'

'Over in the pump-house, washing up for supper. You'd best do the same.' She handed him a clean blue shirt. 'Don't be long; supper's all but ready to set out.' He went tramping out of the kitchen but she called after him, 'What will you do?'

'Let Clayburgh know, an' have him send some of his boys. Smith can ride over to C Star tomorrow, early.' He went on out and down the porch steps, meeting the bony-faced boy, Smith, crossing the yard. 'Supper's about ready. I'll have a job for you first thing

tomorrow. I'll tell you about it directly.'
He walked on into the pump-house.

He had stripped off his sweat-sodden shirt and washed thoroughly, dried himself and pulled on the clean shirt and he was just emerging from the pump-house, shellbelt wrapped around pistol and holster and carried in one hand, when the horsemen arrived in the yard. Even in the diminishing light of the early evening he could recognize them easily enough; Clayburgh, Dave Dehl and a man named Hagan.

Sweat-rimed horses nodding and moving around, they did not dismount, and before Farrer got a chance to say anything, Clayburgh said in his heavy, overbearing voice:

'By God Farrer, yuh got a brass nerve, I'll give yuh that!'

'What?' There had been no mistaking the blunt challenge in Clayburgh's tone, and now, on either side of Clayburgh, Dehl and Hagan were edging their horses wider of him, hands seeking the butts of the pistols they carried, sweating, dirty, hungry no doubt, and in no mood for small-talk. It had been a long and tiring day.

'Dan,' said Dehl,' 'let's just get on with it an' rope the bastard.'

The sounds of the men and the horses had drawn Liz to the yard-door on the porch, Smith appearing quizzically at her shoulder.

'We been trackin' yuh for half this Goddamn' day,' said Clayburgh, 'an' we found the place where some o' my cows is at, Farrer, in a canyon that's well out o'sight an' on your range.'

'You've got off on the wrong foot, Dan,' Farrer said, but Dehl cut in roughly again.

'We don't have to hang around here listenin' to this prick try to tell us that black's white,' he said. 'We seen what we seen. An' we seen this bastard go into that place an' come out again.'

This was well in line with the feeling that Farrer had had, the feeling that he was being watched.

'It's true I found cows belonging to

you,' Farrer said. 'By early tomorrow Smith would have been at your door to say so.'

'You're a liar,' Dehl said, 'an' not a good one at that.'

Farrer's bleak stare found him in the gloom, sensing that Dehl was now very close to pulling the pistol, whatever Clayburgh might think; but Farrer was standing on his own patch of dirt, so he said, not to Dehl but to Clayburgh.

'Your boy here has got a real bad mouth, Dan, so you take him in hand. I know nothin' about how your cows got to where they are. I sure didn't put 'em there an' I don't know who did. Smith didn't put 'em there either; but there's been strangers seen around here, on the hills. Anyway, that's all I've got to say. You just take a crew in whenever you want, an' fetch 'em out, but don't you or any of your shit-mouthed hired help make any accusations you can't back with facts.'

'Back with facts!' Clayburgh sounded even worse than Dehl. For so long he

28

had sought to support his contentions of stolen stock, in the face of what he had perceived to be indifference, even scepticism, and now at last, after a gruelling day in the saddle, here was his vindication, and he was not about to be persuaded otherwise.

'Jesus,' Dehl said. 'We ain't come here to be shit about by some two-bit cow thief off'n a greasy sack outfit like this one! Hage! Get your rope!' And as he said that, Dehl did begin to lift the heavy gun that he wore.

Farrer, however, still holding in his left hand his own holster and shellbelt, got his right one to the butt of his own big Colt very fast and pulled it free, so that Dehl, his gun only partly drawn, was suddenly aware of the long, glinting barrel that Farrer was extending in his direction. There was instant confusion, Liz's voice calling '*Jim!*' the horses shuffling around, and Farrer himself backing away a few paces and calling out to Clayburgh.

'Your boy moves again, he's fly-blown

meat. Now you an' him an' the other clown there, you keep your hands well clear of the weapons. Dan, I told you once I don't know nothin' about your damn' cows; so I want you out o' this yard an' off my place. Whether you go fetch your herd out now or send in a crew tomorrow is all up to you. But now just move on out.'

Clayburgh's horse indeed moved, cutting across anglewise and in the moment that Dehl was screened from Farrer's sight the C Star foreman drew, Farrer sensing it through Liz's sharp cry; but Farrer, already backing further off, blasted a shot above the heads of the horsemen, the flash of the weapon leaping brightly in the yard. Liz Farrer's voice again called something, the C Star men were shouting, Hagan's horse was rearing, and when Dehl managed to get clear and tried to bring his pistol to bear, Farrer was far back in the gloom, near the barn, so that Dehl could not immediately sort out where his target had got to. Limned against the ranch-house lamps behind them, the mounted men were at a dangerous disadvantage.

'Spread out!' yelled Clayburgh. Even as he and his men moved to do so, Liz was coming down the porch steps calling to her husband, Smith following her, the lamplight spilling from the open kitchen door and from the window, picking them out. In a flurry of movement and a thumping and clinking of sound, the yard emptied of horsemen, Clayburgh, Dehl and Hagan spurring away in different directions, soon vanishing into the gathering night; but they did not go far, it seemed, for they could be heard calling to each other, obviously preparing to stake out the barn, where they believed Farrer to be, Liz, going towards the same place, said in a low, urgent voice:

'Jim?'

He was still there, right enough, and he had got the saddle up on his horse and was now attending to the cinches. Somewhere out in the darkness a gun

31

flashed and something hit an outbuilding close to the barn.

'Get down!' hissed Farrer. Smith had already hit the ground and was crawling towards the tall open doors, while Liz, running inside, collided with Farrer, clutching at him.

'Jim, you can't just up and run! That's the same as telling Clayburgh you did rustle his stock!'

He took her by the shoulders. 'Liz, listen. Just listen to me. You saw them an' heard what they said. The mood they're in, if I don't get out of here an' give 'em time to cool off, then in less than five minutes I'll be swingin' from that hoist-beam up there. I've got to buy some time. Maybe you should get word to George Wenlake.' Before she could answer, he swung up into the saddle and after that he wasted no time at all with more talk. Yelling at the already tired horse, driving spurs in, crouching low over its neck, Farrer went charging out of the barn and across the open yard. In the outer gloom, somebody — Dehl perhaps — shouted.

'The bastard's on the move!' Immediately there came another heavy gunshot, the flick of flame over to Farrer's left, but he was now out beyond the glow of the house-lamps and he had the advantage of knowing where obstacles lay as he urged the chestnut on.

Nevertheless, it did not take Clayburgh and his men long to rally and come together again and set out after the hard-riding Farrer. Liz heard them still shouting to each other, and she stood in the yard near the barn, one hand pressed to her throat, her breathing laboured, a dull ache beginning in her temples as the reaction to the shock and urgency and the shooting set in. So this was it; the end. After all their struggles and all their disappointments. It was as though some malevolent deity had singled them out, marked them for failure, and it seemed to be the realization of all her worst fears, the culmination of all her brooding dissatisfaction over recent times.

3

Garrick's freight yard in Blayrock was extensive and surrounded by raw wooden buildings, an office with living-quarters attached to it at the back, assorted outbuildings for storage of equipment, a barn, a long structure with flap-fronted horse stalls, a pump-house, a small bunkhouse separated slightly from the rest and standing at the far end of the yard; and an area board-fenced on one side where stood a third flat-deck wagon, and with space there for two other wagons. All this was situated on a side-street running off Main and customary access was in off that street; but there was another outlet to a back street that ran parallel with Main.

Garrick's yard-boy was Lem Alford, and it was he who was now engaged in transferring what freight now remained on Garrick's wagon to the one that had been driven in by Steve Elder. Next, Alford would unharness both of the teams and lead them away to be fed and watered; and early next day, behind other, fresh horses, Elder would drive on, alone, to Georgeville and Bannock.

By this time, however, Garrick had washed up and changed his shirt and was now in the kitchen along at Wenlake's. Emily's greeting had been warm but foreshortened, for her father, who was Blayrock County Sheriff, had come clumping along from his front office, through the passageway to the kitchen, only moments after Garrick had arrived.

'Wes is here for supper,' Emily said, cheeks flushed from going busily about her tasks, and there were appetizing smells coming from several pots set out on the glowing stove. Ten years younger than Garrick, she was a slim but neatly-rounded woman of just a little above medium height, with shining dark hair and intensely blue eyes and with a short, straight nose; not a beautiful woman, but a strikingly pretty one, and who had a soft, fluid way of moving.

Although Wenlake nodded to Garrick, his face was without particular expression, Garrick knowing full well that, just short of dislike, the dour Wenlake's opinion of him was still far from an approving one, and Garrick had his own views on the chief reason for that.

Wenlake was not quite as tall as Garrick, a slim, sharp-featured man nearing fifty, with prominent cheekbones, ruddy-coloured skin stretched over them, sandy hair and a neatly-clipped, fair moustache. For what it was worth, Garrick mentioned the conversation he had had with the rancher, Clayburgh.

'Oh, yeah, he's been here too,' Wenlake said, 'on again about some damn' cows that he claims is missin'; him an' Dave Dehl an' that other feller, Hagan, all tearin' here an' there an' back again like whiskey-fired Apaches.' Emily glanced at him, then back to what she was doing. 'Where was it you run across him?'

'About five miles from here,' said Garrick. 'Clayburgh was considering putting the hard word on some neighbours.'

'What?' Wenlake now showed a touch more interest, perhaps even slight concern when that was mentioned. 'You mean Bolt?'

'Bolt's been up in Benning Forks an' I told Clayburgh that; but yeah, Bolt. Farrer too, so he said.'

This time Emily shot a quick look at Garrick, then away; but Wenlake had noticed, and said in a way that Garrick had come to recognize and dislike, for it was not too far short of a sneer:

'Your good friends.'

Garrick simply nodded. 'I advised him to tread light if he decided to ride out to the Flying F, shooting his mouth off.'

'Did you now?' said Wenlake. 'Did you now? An' do you seriously think that Dan Clayburgh's about to take advice from you?'

'Probably not,' said Garrick. 'Dave Dehl sure wouldn't, anyway.'

From a rack above the stove Emily took warmed plates and softly shoo-ed her way to the table to begin setting them out. If she had hoped that, through the interruption, Wenlake would allow the matter to rest, she was to be disappointed, even when she also said: 'Pa, by the time you've washed up, supper will be all ready.'

'I sure hope,' Wenlake said to Garrick, 'that you didn't plan on backin' up this advice o' yours by somehow shovin' your oar in, as well.'

'If I do,' Garrick said, for Emily's sake holding his irritation in check, 'I'll be sure to let you know, George, even if it's after.'

'What you'd be a long way better off doin',' Wenlake said, a deeper flush invading his cheeks, 'is what you do best, keep right on haulin' freight an' leave range problems out on the range where they belong.'

'Pa — ' Emily began.

'All right Em,' said Wenlake, 'I'll go wash up now. But I ain't done with this yet.' He turned abruptly and walked out.

Emily looked wanly at Garrick, for clearly this was to be another meal at which tension intruded and which would likely end with another niggly argument between her father and Garrick, altogether another blighted evening. When Wenlake had gone, Garrick said:

'I'm sorry Em. I'd have been smarter just not mentioning it.'

'And be blamed later, maybe, for holding something back?' She knew her father's tactics well and it was not only the heat from the stove that was causing the flush in her cheeks; and she fell silent as she went about dishing up the meal and making sure there would be coffee on hand. With slim fingers she indicated a chair and Garrick walked across and sat down to await Wenlake's reappearance.

The meal was eaten in an awkward, loaded silence, but surprisingly, even when it was over and coffee had been drunk, Wenlake did not raise the matter again but scraped his chair back and stood up.

'That was a real good meal, Em. Now I'm goin' back up to the office an' get some paperwork done.' Without another glance at Garrick, he went stumping out and presently a far door slammed; but for a time they could hear him moving around, opening and closing drawers; then things went quiet.

Emily sighed and propped her chin on clasped hands.

'It gets no better, Wes. In fact, I think it gets worse.'

'And you know why as well as I do.'

'Wes — '

'If you left here, what would he do? He'd be lost. No cook, no housekeeper. Em, you're locked to him just as though he'd put manacles on you.'

All this they had traversed before, over and over. If, now, she did acknowledge to herself the reality of what he was saying, she would resist doing so aloud, at least unless he continued to press the matter, compelling her to say something. Yet in the end, arguing it all over again would serve no purpose, for in the past they had always come full circle. The only difference that it ever made was that the division created by this repeated question of George Wenlake's motives, grew slightly wider. They always lost something, Emily and Garrick; Wenlake lost nothing. And on the fringes of this oft-trodden path lay another, much less defined matter of dissent, the Farrers; and perhaps the most distasteful aspect of that was that it did not quite emerge into the light, tending to remain in darker, unspoken realms of discontent, the worse for being concealed, surfacing only at times through a particular glance, a certain veiled expression that Garrick had come to believe could amount to but one thing; mistrust of him. Tonight, though, had George

Wenlake come within a split second of fetching it into the open? '*Your good friends.*' Not the words, but the way they had been spoken and the supercilious look that had accompanied them; for it had not been both of the Farrers that had been on Wenlake's mind. For some little while there had been rumours abroad that Jim and Liz Farrer had begun to drift apart. County gossips spoke of a rift between them. Wes Garrick happened to be the closest friend the Farrers had, but he would never be drawn on the subject; and indeed neither of the Farrers had ever broached the matter, even to Garrick, always maintaining at least an outward show of normal domestic life. Tongues, however, had begun to link him with Liz Farrer, and the talk had long ago reached Wenlake, who had lost no time in airing it for what he saw as his daughter's best interests. '*You're wastin' your time with that feller, Em.*' And then: '*Don't you come, later, sayin' I didn't tell you.*' Of course she had defended Garrick, for she was not only defending a man whose integrity she had come to believe in, she was defending her own choice of man, her own good sense.

Garrick, for he had also become well aware of the talk, if not all of its substance, came close to confronting that whole issue, here and now, getting it all out on the table once and for all, for it would have reached Emily by some means, of that he felt quite certain; so there could be no point in pussy-footing around it. Yet something he was not able quite to define held him back. Perhaps he himself did not want to confront it. *Was* there, at least on the part of Liz Farrer, a real, though indeed unarticulated attraction to Garrick? Occasionally he had felt that her manner had at least brushed that possibility. Was it that, having begun to draw away from Jim Farrer, she had been tempted to look for consolation elsewhere, reaching out perhaps, for reassurance, rather than anything more substantial than that?

In the finish, and though the perfect opportunity had been there, Garrick did not obey his initial impulse to broach this sensitive subject with Emily. It was a decision he would come to regret. She had produced some sewing from a cane basket and bent over her task. Conversation was desultory for Wenlake had left his mark on the evening, though the man himself had not reappeared. Finally Garrick rose and said he had best be going, and without mentioning any of his concerns over the Farrers and the possible visit to the Flying F of the fiery and unpredictable Clayburgh. Something else concealed, perhaps also to come back to haunt him at some future time.

Then, as Emily too, stood up, laying aside her sewing they heard Wenlake's voice, along with someone else's — a man's — the second one sounding agitated. Garrick would not have delayed leaving, but almost at once, Wenlake could be heard walking along the passageway and he came into the kitchen trailed somewhat diffidently by a young cowhand whom Garrick recognized immediately as Smith, Jim Farrer's remaining hired hand. The youngster was carrying his hat in his hand and was wearing range clothing, with a short, thickly-lined jacket over his brown shirt, and in spite of it, looked hunched with cold from his night ride, his narrow face ruddy from the chill of the night air.

Wenlake, a curious expression on his face, said to Garrick: 'Ah, you're still here. Well, you'll be interested in this. Your great friend Farrer is now in some kind o' real trouble.' To Smith, he said: 'You say it.'

Though he appeared to be uncomfortable at being the centre of attention and kept lowering his eyes, the cowhand did so, and he ended by saying:

'It was real bad. Dan Clayburgh, he was fit to spit iron, an' when Mr Farrer put one over their heads, they split up fast an' then they started shootin' up the barn, where he'd gone.'

Garrick said; 'Finding C Star cattle on the Flying F, apart from a few strays, doesn't make any kind of sense.'

'It seems it didn't make sense to Clayburgh, neither,' said Wenlake.

Garrick did not even glance at him, but, to get the matter straight in his own mind, said to Smith; 'I just can't see Jim Farrer firing a shot without having good reason. What was it drove him to that?'

Smith shrugged, but said: 'It was kinda hard to see all the moves but it seemed to me that Dave Dehl, he started to pull his own iron, an' then the horses moved an' Mr Farrer shot an' went backin' away so he got hisself into a darker place, an' Hagan's horse stood near on its — ' flicking a confused glance at Emily, 'on its tail, an' by the time they got settled down, Mr Farrer, he'd got hisself into the barn. So that's when they piled on out o' that yard *muy pronto* an' split up. Then Mr Farrer come out o' that barn mounted up, an' got out across the yard an' they shot at him an' then lit out after him. I dunno what happened after that. Nobody come back.'

Garrick's next question was quiet but firm and was the one that made Emily look at him, and made Wenlake do so as well.

'Liz — Mrs Farrer, is she all right?'

'Yeah. Oh yeah. It was her sent me in to tell Mr Wenlake.'

Garrick turned his attention to Wenlake. 'What will you do?'

For a moment Wenlake simply continued staring at Garrick, but then he said: 'Do? Well, I can tell you what I *ain't* about to do, an' that's go harin' off all over Farrer's range shoutin' out for the owner. Clayburgh'll catch up with him or he won't. Either way, I'll get to hear about it.'

'If they take him,' Garrick said, 'they'll likely lynch him. You heard what Smith said.'

He heard Emily's faint intake of breath.

'There's nothin' I can do about that,'

said Wenlake. 'I doubt they could hear me shoutin' from this distance.'

In spite of the man's flippancy, there could be no arguing with the logic of what he was saying. Emily's face, however, betrayed the question she could not bring herself to ask of Garrick. '*What will you do?*' Instead she turned to the stove, saying to Smith: 'Sit down, won't you? I'll pour you some coffee.'

It was at that point that Garrick took the opportunity to reach for his hat and bid them all goodnight. He went out, Wenlake's sardonic gaze following him, the ravaged look on Emily's face lingering in his mind long after he had gone.

4

By early morning they were in town, Clayburgh, Dehl and Hagan, tired, bad tempered and hungry. They did not go rapping on the door of any eatery or rooming-house, however, but got stiffly down from their head-hanging horses in the yard in the back of Hesse's big saloon, a place which went by no other name except Hesse's.

Hesse himself had heard them coming into the yard and had looked out, a thickset man of fifty with a nearly-bald head and a pouchy face, putting on steel-rimmed eyeglasses, the better to see who it was down there; and when he did see who it was, he went one heavy step at a time down the stairs, calling out for the big man, Ryder, to stir himself.

Well over six feet tall, built like a lumberjack, his stubbly face still pouched and lined with sleep, naked, curled hair growing out of his groin to a thick, dark mat on his chest, Ryder had left the black-haired woman, Maria, mumbling and groping in the large, rumpled bed, when he went to answer Hesse.

'Wha's goin' on?' asked Ryder.

'I dunno,' said Hesse, now going down the back hall, 'but half o' the C Star is in the yard lookin' fit to drop, so somethin's up, for sure.' Hesse's face was set seriously for he was a man who believed that he could detect trouble a long way off without anybody having to draw any diagrams for him. Over his shoulder he called to Ryder: 'Stir Maria out of that pit an' have her fix some chow.'

Garrick was in his freight yard checking the horses, moving from stall to stall, gently working and smoothing hands down veined legs, examining each animal critically. When finally he crossed the yard on the way back to the kitchen, the boy, Lem Alford, gangly and pale, came scuffing out of the bunkhouse.

'In ten minutes we'll fix breakfast,' called Garrick, and then he instructed the boy about which of the horses were to be used for the one wagon that was to be taken on to Georgeville and beyond. 'Give Steve a call.' Alford nodded and went tramping back towards the bunkhouse. A strange, taciturn young man, he had come through Blayrock about a year ago, homeless, ragged, seeking odd jobs sufficient to feed and clothe himself and pay for somewhere to sleep. He had said that he was sixteen years old, though Garrick had judged him to be all of fourteen, and had debated a good while on the wisdom of hiring him. In the finish, more than a little influenced by Emily, whose heart had gone out to the lone boy, Garrick had taken him on for what he had clearly stipulated was to be a month's trial. Alford, however, had proven his worth, being quick to learn and, belying his somewhat slouching appearance, meticulous in all the duties

51

that Garrick laid out for him. Even the often-hard-to-please Elder had had to give his grudging approval; and there could be no doubt that the freight yard had seen benefits from having somebody always around when Garrick and Elder were away. A third driver, Maylor, had shown himself to be addicted to the bottle and too attracted to other people's property and had been sent on his way; and Garrick was under no illusions that ever since, Lem Alford had been eyeing the immobile wagon in the yard in the hope of one day being assigned to drive it. So far, Garrick had simply said: 'When work picks up, we'll see.' Ruefully, Garrick now thought that if he were to become involved even marginally in this situation that had developed out of the Flying F (and he felt strongly that he owed support to those who had supported and encouraged him) the day when young Alford did have to take the reins, even if only as a temporary measure, might not be very far off.

What Smith had told them of events out on the Farrer ranch had troubled Garrick deeply and now that shots had actually been fired he knew that it would need an almost superhuman effort to restore even a semblance of sanity. He had seen other such situations arise, over cattle, in other places, and had seen them get right out of control very quickly, and usually end in bloodshed. Over recent hours his thoughts had turned again to Liz Farrer, now virtually alone out on the Flying F, though he had not been without a pang of regret when he thought, too, of the look that had been on Emily's face last night when he had been leaving. Alford came out of the bunkhouse and went towards the privy. Garrick went up the steps and into the kitchen.

It was in fact young Alford, a little later that morning, having been out along Main, who had walked past Sheriff Wenlake outside the jail office and talking with Clayburgh.

'I'm goin' nowhere but to get my

Goddamn' head down for a coupla hours,' Clayburgh had been saying.

'Notwithstandin', I'll say it to you again,' Alford had heard Wenlake say; 'I've got a chore to do that can't wait, outside of Blayrock, but let's you an' me get this clear; when I get back I don't want to hear that you or Dave Dehl — him in particular — has gone out there again lookin' for Farrer. If the facts, when I get to hear 'em all, tell me that a posse has to be got up, then I'll be the one to do that.'

Alford, passing beyond them, had heard no more, but what he had heard he had passed on to Garrick who had been out in the yard, having just seen Elder on his way to Georgeville. Now, however, Garrick had a number of routine tasks to attend to before coming to a final decision on whether or not he would ride out to the Flying F. At least, from what Alford had just told him, Jim Farrer was in no immediate danger, Wenlake having given Dan Clayburgh the straight message about that; but

Garrick, calling the boy back now, said: 'First job this afternoon, get the saddle horse checked over, ready for me. It might be that I'll need him.'

Hesse, as seemed to be expected, had found accommodation for the men from C Star in a couple of back rooms, and by about noon they were up again and moving around, stretching and scratching, and by now looking for something to drink.

Less than half an hour later they were all in the long bar of the saloon with Hesse, Clayburgh and Hagan talking with several cowmen, all of whom were disturbed to hear of the proven theft of C Star stock. Dehl was deep in low-voiced conversation with Hesse. A lean, whipcord man leaning on the bar, a man with a prominent Adam's apple and a cast in one eye, said to Clayburgh:

'I'm but a pilgrim, as you might say, but it sure does rile me to hear o' this here thievin' that you say is goin' on. There's no denyin' that times is hard, but all up an' down the damn' country there's plenty o' folks that's hurtin' that ain't yet come down to thievin' from their neighbours.'

Clayburgh, unshaven, his mind still dulled through not enough sleep, and like his companions, stale with old sweat, nodded heavily.

'That's just about it, mister. But if it had been scum from outside this country, passin' through, well, that'd be one thing; but this bastard's stood where you are, sinkin' drinks I paid for, an' once, he sat at my board, an' by God I'll not forgive this. I didn't keep a-hold o' that spread o' mine out there, through all the shit in Creation, to have the fruits o' that labour run off into somebody else's canyon.'

'An' the law here?' the lean man enquired. 'What does the law here plan on doin' about it? Assumin' o' course that there is some?'

'Wenlake,' said Clayburgh. 'He's due back later an' he reckons he'll be lookin' for the facts; but by God if George seems as though he's draggin' his boots

56

an' questionin' this an' that an' hemmin' an' hawin', then I'll whip up my own posse an' comb that Goddamn' range 'til I run the bastard down.' There was a general murmuring of approval at that, for it was the sort of talk that other cowmen liked to hear. 'In any case,' Clayburgh said then, 'I'll be takin' a crew in there to fetch my cows an' if I catch sight o' that thievin' little shit while I'm about it, all his luck is gonna run out real quick.' For a moment, Clayburgh's eyes rested on Bolt, but although he still deeply mistrusted the ruddy-faced man, and in particular when he seemed to have ample money for liquor, Clayburgh appeared to be resigned to the fact that, if the man ever had been involved in rustling C Star cattle, then this time he was probably in the clear. Yet Clayburgh's eye would never shift away from Bolt for long, for he was part of a long-standing theory.

Dave Dehl, however, leaving a grim-looking Hesse and now mingling with others, passed close by Clayburgh, muttering: 'There's that bastard Bolt. The freighter saw him in Benning Forks, spendin', an' now here he is.'

'Let it be, for now,' Clayburgh said. 'We'll likely get back to Bolt.'

Hesse had got up too and come nearer, overhearing and sourly agreeing. 'He'll lift anything you don't have roped down is my opinion. An' Farrer would've needed help shiftin' your beef.'

'Well,' said Clayburgh, 'that's some-thin' we might yet have to come back to. Farrer maybe did have help. I'd say, yeah, he'd have to. But I reckon the stuff was goin' in there a few head at a time, 'til recent times, when there was a bigger herd moved. That woulda needed help. Oh, we'll sure come back to Mister Bolt; but first we'll have Farrer nailed.'

Nearby, Hagan, at one of the small wooden tables, held up a fresh bottle, and Dave Dehl nodded and crossed to him and sat down, to be joined by the large and ugly Ryder, Hesse's man, all of them clearly settling in for a session. As far as Dehl and Hagan were concerned yesterday had been a long day followed by a longer night and all to no satisfactory result, having lost their quarry in the near-moonless dark.

By early in the afternoon Garrick had decided that he must go out to the Flying F to find out if Jim Farrer had been seen, or if not, whether Liz had any idea of where he might have headed. Perhaps he had said something to her that Smith had not heard. Now, however, he had been along to McCoy's feed and grain to settle up an account, but he was still full of thoughts about the Farrers. Smith, he knew, had headed right back to the ranch, but Smith was only a youngster and in all likelihood would not be asked to put himself in jeopardy should matters take another ugly turn. Angling across Main, Garrick did not immediately notice the C Star rider, Hagan, on the boardwalk outside Hesse's saloon until Hagan, his craggy face aglow from the drinking he had been doing, called out:

'Hey there, wagon-man, how's about your scumbag *compadre* now? Yuh been rubbin' knees with any other cow thieves we didn't know about?' Garrick considered simply walking on, not offering Hagan the satisfaction of provoking anger, but then, belching, the man said: 'No matter, I reckon. Good chance for yuh to give that purty li'l mare out there another tickle.'

Garrick, striding along easily, simply changed direction slightly and, un-armed as he was, hands swinging loosely, was suddenly within three paces of the man on the boardwalk. Hagan, whose reactions had lost some of their edge, even so dropped a rawboned hand to the butt of his old, slung pistol, but found that a pair of powerful fists had reached up and he had been seized by the front of his shirt and jerked forward, fetching him off balance. Drawing the gun was forgotten, as instinctively Hagan reached forward with his own hands in an effort to save himself. Yet he was virtually lifted off the boardwalk and as he came forward, Garrick's right forearm chopped across catching Hagan on the right cheekbone, slamming his head sideways. Hagan went down hard, rolling over and over in the dust of the street, his hat tumbling away.

People on Main paused to watch. Presently, Hagan, his nose bleeding freely, got up on his hands and knees and it was at that stage that he remembered the gun he was carrying, and for a second time he made to grasp the butt of it. Garrick's boot struck Hagan's right elbow and produced a yell of pain, and Hagan collapsed, grabbing at the elbow with his other hand.

'Make to pull that iron again,' Garrick said, 'an' I'll sink another boot in so you'll be of no more use to any Blayrock whore.'

Garrick would have left him there but at that moment the batwing doors of Hesse's were pushed open and Dave Dehl, followed by Ryder, Clayburgh, a swaying Nathan Bolt, the tall, cast-eyed pilgrim and several others all came crowding out to look at what had happened to Hagan.

'What's this?' demanded Clayburgh.

'This is what happens to an imitation hard man who can't keep a halter on his mouth,' said Garrick. 'He's one of yours, so you take him in hand before he makes another mistake an' finds he's never going to walk upright again.'

'We don't have to take shit like this from some two-bit freight hauler,' Dehl said. He dropped down off the boardwalk, landing lightly for such a thickset, heavy-looking man, and the big fellow from Hesse's, Ryder, stepped down behind him.

More people had come out to Main, some of them merely curious, some fearful, others no doubt eagerly anticipating further violence, and all at someone else's expense. Garrick knew from the start that this was to be as much directed at Farrer as at himself, Clayburgh's party having failed publicly to come up with Farrer; but now they could send a message to him by taking apart his friend, Garrick.

'No shotgun today,' Dave Dehl observed.

'Count that as real good luck,' said Garrick, 'otherwise, you could still be up there on that boardwalk tryin' to push your gut back in the hole.'

Dehl did not say more, but at once swung a club-like blow at Garrick, one that, as he weaved to one side, ripped the air just a fraction of an inch from his head. Voices were now calling out, Bolt's whiskey-fired one prominent among them.

'Cut the bastard down Dave!'

'Could be he's in it with Farrer!'

'Kick the shit out of him Dave!'

Clearly the minds of all the range men who happened to be in Blayrock on this day had become focused on the theft of Clayburgh's cattle, and their mood was one of retribution, a lashing out at somebody — anybody — who could have even the most tenuous connection with it. This was the kind of crowd now building behind Dehl and Ryder that could quite easily become a mob capable, ultimately, of mindless acts. Hagan had gone crawling away but was now sitting with his back against the boardwalk, his lower face masked with blood from his nose and slowly trying to flex his still-deadened right arm.

When Dehl again swung his fist and once more failed to make contact with the fast-moving Garrick, Garrick hit him hard with his left fist and snapped the C Star foreman's head to one side, fetching a sharp cry from him; then Garrick pumped another jab that caught Dehl in the right eye socket and caused him to go stepping backward in pain, shaking his head, trying to see where Garrick was.

By now, however, Ryder had closed on Garrick and ripped in a punch which could not be avoided, and this time pain seared Garrick as Ryder's big fist impacted on his left rib cage, belting him sideways. Truly, this man of Hesse's was a powerful puncher, getting his weight in behind a blow in the style of a trained fighter, punching not merely with his arms as Dehl had done, wasting energy. Again closing, Ryder hit Garrick with two rapid blows, driving him back, then down, rolling him in the street, dust rising, blood on his mouth. Dehl, recovering, saw his opportunity and ran forward, kicking at Garrick, but Garrick, seeing him just in time, kept rolling, then came to his knees.

'Leave the bastard to me Dave,' Ryder said. 'I'll put 'im away real *pronto.*'

Garrick came struggling to his feet, his head ringing, his hands hurting, realizing that he was not strong enough, nor in all probability good enough to withstand an onslaught from Ryder, but made up his mind that he would not turn away from the man. If Ryder wanted to, he would have to take him the hard way.

They went weaving and crouching and lashing out at one another, circling in the middle of the street now, voices still calling out to them, more people arriving, faces at most of the windows. Finally, Ryder, moving with surprising speed, came in on Garrick, pounding hard, bashing through his defences, catching him on shoulder and cheek in quick succession, hammering him to his knees by means of sheer, savage strength. Garrick knew that it was all over, that he would now receive a bad beating at the hands of this hulking man; and there would be nothing now that he could do about it.

Somebody then fired a Colt, the sound of it booming on Main, and all heads turned to see George Wenlake walking along towards them, also in the middle of the street, the long pistol still held high above his head. Even Ryder paused in his advance towards Garrick; and Dehl, who had been angling to get behind Garrick, stopped and looked towards the peace officer.

'Whatever it's about,' Wenlake said, coming to where they were, still in a film of dust, 'break it up right now an' clear this street.' He was wagging the glinting barrel of the pistol to encourage the bystanders to disperse, and with some show of disappointment, they began to do so. Hesse, standing holding the batwing doors of his saloon, jerked his round head at Ryder who, with a last malevolent glance at Garrick who was getting to his feet, turned away. Before following Ryder, however, Dave Dehl paused.

'There'll come another day wagonman. Believe it.'

When they had gone, the sour and still bleeding Hagan with them, Wenlake asked Garrick: 'What the hell was all that about? Farrer?'

'More or less. Me an' Hagan had words. Dehl an' Ryder bought in.'

'You bit off more'n you could chew in a month,' Wenlake observed. 'I'll tell you what I told Clayburgh. Keep right out of it unless I give the word. Now you go haul your freight. It's what you do for a livin'.' He turned on his heel and walked away.

Aching deeply from the blows he had taken, Garrick picked up his hat which had fallen off during the fight, put it on and went slowly along in the direction of his freight yard. One thing he had firmly made up his mind about — or had had it made up for him through the one remark passed by Hagan — and that was that he would go out to the Flying F, principally to assure himself that Liz Farrer would be forewarned of the danger she might be in from men such as Hagan and Dehl, especially now that popular anger was being whipped up around Blayrock. Emily also came into his thoughts, however, and he knew that he might well be putting their future in jeopardy when inevitably she came to know what he was doing.

5

Water was streaming from him as, stripped to the waist, he bent over a large bowl, sluicing dirt and blood away, wetting all of his head in the process; then he towelled hair, face, neck and torso before putting on a clean shirt. His head was aching, his left cheekbone and his lower lip felt painful, his skinned knuckles smarted, and the deep pain still probed his left rib-cage. Nonetheless, he had to admit that his injuries would have been infinitely greater had not George Wenlake shown up when he did.

Lem Alford, hovering just outside in the yard, had seen some of the fighting from a distance and had not known what to do. If he had respected Garrick before this, indeed he now stared through the open doorway at him in a way that was little short of awe, for

69

neither the boy nor, for that matter, anyone else in Blayrock could have conceived of any man, on his own, not only knocking down somebody like Hagan, but then standing his ground in front of Dave Dehl and the truly frightening Ryder. It had come then as a revelation to Alford, as it must have done to those numerous others, for the man who ran this freight line had always seemed to be a quiet, even retiring individual, certainly not a man to go out of his way to seek trouble.

Presently, however, Alford, at the door, said: 'I got him ready, Mr Garrick, with the blanket on, but he ain't saddled yet. You still need him? He's still in the barn.'

'Maybe,' said Garrick. Then: 'Yeah, you might as well throw the saddle on him; but for now he can stay in the barn.'

Alford went scuffing away. Garrick still had an odd, uncertain feeling about going out on the Flying F and he wished that George Wenlake had been more precise about what he intended doing, provided he was persuaded by Clayburgh that something needed to be done. One thing, though, was certain; Garrick himself had no intention of raising the matter with the man. *'Now you go haul your freight. It's what you do for a livin'.'* That comment, true though it undeniably was, took no account of personal feelings, of friendships or of perceived loyalties. Yet even as the word loyalties came into his mind, so too did Emily. Nevertheless he compelled himself to consider with a greater degree of logic, exactly what he ought to do if he did go out onto the Farrer ranch. His earliest impulse had been to ride directly out to the ranch-house, to where Liz would be; but from the back of his mind something else now emerged for consideration. Perhaps there was just a possibility that he might first be able to make contact with Farrer himself, always provided the man had not already returned to the ranch-house. Garrick had remembered

71

that at a certain place near to the western line between the Flying F and C Star, there was a ramshackle, sun-curled structure that once had been used by Flying F as a line shack in the days when Farrer had been able to afford to employ several hands. Maybe, gambling that no one would believe he would choose to hole up in a place so close to C Star range, Farrer might have done exactly that. Garrick had to smile faintly when the thought came to him, for indeed it would be typical of Jim Farrer to make such a move, treading to the very edge of danger.

Earlier, Garrick had brought the repeating shotgun inside the house, and though he had no intention at all of going armed, now, out of long habit, he unloaded the gun to examine each of the waxy-red cartridges with their bright brass caps; for if such a weapon were to be left loaded and untouched for a while, it was possible for cartridges to deteriorate through heat or damp or general humidity. All of the loads he removed, however, were in mint condition. He knew he had no need to look through the barrel of the gun for evidence of leading for he always gave attention to that at the first opportunity after the gun had been used. Now, he did not reload the gun but closed it up and placed it on its wall-pegs, then put the five cartridges into a waxboard box containing others, replacing the box in a nearby cupboard.

Hardly had he completed this routine than he became aware of someone in the yard, and when he stepped to the door, discovered that it was Emily Wenlake. He stood to one side as she came up the steps and inside.

'Pa told me what happened,' Emily said. 'Are you all right Wes?'

'Somewhat bruised here an' there,' he said. 'If George hadn't come along when he did it could have been a whole lot worse.'

Slim fingers softly brushed the angry swelling on the side of his face. 'Why, Wes? What happened?'

Garrick shrugged, not wanting to bring Liz Farrer's name into it. 'It was the man, Hagan, from C Star, half drunk, lettin' his mouth run away with him. They've been down at Hesse's all day.'

'Wes, it isn't at all like you to get mixed up in a town brawl.'

'Sometimes it happens that you're not left much room to move. It happened today.'

Emily's deep blue eyes regarded him intently and he felt that she might be reading more into his words. Then she said: 'He's talking about getting up a posse to go out and look for Jim Farrer.' When Garrick made no immediate comment she said: 'You have to understand, Wes, that he hasn't really been left with an option. After all he is the Blayrock County sheriff and he's been handed a serious complaint; and the man accused hasn't helped himself by running off the way he did. What else can Pa do?'

'I didn't say he could do otherwise,

Em,' said Garrick, 'but I don't put a whole lot of weight on the fact that Jim Farrer made sure he got to put some distance between himself an' C Star. Whether Clayburgh would've stopped it or not I don't know, but Dave Dehl an' Hagan, they'd have lynched Jim, believe it. If that had happened, George an' his authority wouldn't have counted for anything; it would've been too late for that. Dan Clayburgh's only here in Blayrock laying his complaint now because him an' his boys lost track of Jim.' He had not raised his voice but there was no mistaking his disdain for Dehl and Hagan in particular, no matter what the circumstances.

Knowing that what he had said was more than likely true, she had lowered her gaze, but now, looking up again, she said: 'I realize it wouldn't have been right for them to take the law into their own hands like that. Those times are supposed to be behind us. But they *did* find C Star cattle on the Flying F range, and it wasn't just a matter of a few strays. You can't defend *that*, Wes, no matter how you try.'

'I'm not about to try,' he said. 'But finding them there doesn't prove that Jim Farrer put them there; an' he'd have struggled to have done it on his own, an' nobody's yet accused young Smith of rustling. Ask George.'

Still she could not — or would not — concede, reflecting George Wenlake, no doubt, at his most persuasive. Yet she surprised Garrick when suddenly she said: 'Why don't you go out with the posse? Knowing Jim so well, you might be able to help; help Jim, I mean.'

Garrick looked at her levelly. 'Where do you think he'll find the men for this posse of his? Who do you think will go? When you come down to it, he doesn't have a lot of choices; an' I'll not ride ten yards with the sweepings from Hesse's saloon, law or no law, George or no George.'

The faint flush that came into her cheeks told him that she had been stung by that, as though recognition of this truth reflected in an unflattering way upon her father. Garrick had not intended to sound as harsh as he now realized he must have done. But it was too late and just sufficient to trigger a quick response from her.

'It's really *her*, isn't it? Liz.'

'No.'

'Now you're not concerned about her? Last night I got a different impression.'

'Yes. Yes, I'm concerned. I'm as concerned as I'd want any friend of mine to be about you if things were the other way about.'

At this moment more than any other, by the expression on her face, he knew that she no longer believed him, and in the space of another second she confirmed it and he could have cursed aloud, almost hearing George Wenlake's voice uttering the words.

'Wes, you've known Liz Farrer for a long while, in fact for longer than you've known me. There was something between you, wasn't there? Don't think that I haven't noticed, whenever she's been here in Blayrock, the way she looks at you sometimes. I don't like being deceived Wes. I'd rather you'd be honest with me, no matter what the consequences.'

He had to draw a long breath in an effort to rein in his anger.

'Em, that's just not so.'

'If it isn't, then promise me that you'll keep right away from the Flying F. Let Pa take his posse out.'

Now, when it was too late, Garrick saw that she had sprung the trap on him, so that he would have to agree with her or earn her anger. Or deceive her. Looking at her intently, he said: 'Em, if there's anything at all worthwhile between you an' me, you have to trust me over this. I can't believe that Jim's done what they're saying he's done. He's been a good friend to me. I owe it to him to at least hear him out, no matter what Clayburgh says. Or George.'

Her cheeks were burning now. 'You

don't have to say any more Wes. You do what you like. Remember though, that it's you who has to face up to whatever might happen.' Before he could say any more to her she had turned and left him, going down the steps and into the yard.

6

Within sight of the shack, through patches of brush, Garrick brought his black horse to a halt. From where he had stopped he was not able to see the entire structure but he could see enough to cast some doubt on the wisdom of his coming to this place. The building had not totally collapsed but parts of its roof seemed to have fallen in and one of the age-grey wooden walls was beginning to sag inwards.

With his knees Garrick nudged the black and walked him, weaving in and out between clumps of brush, taking care to avoid scraping against razor-like thorns, and began making a slow, complete circuit of the line shack. By the time he got all of the way around he was convinced of one thing at least; there was no evidence of an occupant and no horse anywhere in sight. Again

Garrick drew his own horse to a halt, sitting still in the saddle. A small breeze had sprung up, stirring dust through this dry strip of country which lay like an ochre-coloured scar through the greener rangelands, a place where the coarse, ragged and ugly brush had established itself. Now he was unsure of what he ought to do next, but he had come as far as this and believed that, although the place seemed to be deserted, he should at least go through the motions of checking it out. So again he moved the black forward, passing between parched brush, and when he got to within thirty feet of the shack, he swung down. Softly, he called: 'Jim? Jim Farrer?' He waited. There was no reply. Leading the horse by the reins he then walked forward towards the door that was hanging by one hinge and standing partly open. When he got to the doorway he could see enough of the interior to confirm that the place was indeed quite empty. That was when he heard the pistol cock and stood motionless. Then Farrer's voice said: 'Turn around.' Garrick turned slowly. Farrer was perhaps thirty feet from him, standing in a half crouch, long pistol drawn and lined up steadily; but the instant that Farrer realized who it was, he straightened up and at the same time lowered the big Colt. 'Christ Wes, I didn't reckon it bein' you.' The Colt was slid back into its holster and Farrer walked across and they gripped hands. 'You're a sight for sore eyes,' Farrer said, 'but what in the name of God are you doin', pokin' around 'way out here?'

'Like half the county will be, by this time,' said Garrick, 'looking to find you. Yours is the name on everybody's tongue. I came here on a hunch an' I'd just got resigned to the fact I'd made a mistake, outsmarted myself, more like. Where were you?'

'Oh, I'd been holed up in there,' Farrer said. 'Saw your dust though.' He moved his head slightly. 'I've got the horse picketed out there in the brush. This is the kind of place that sends out its own signals when company's on the way.'

Garrick nodded. Then: 'This whole thing is one hell of a mess Jim.' He told him about Smith coming into Blayrock to see Wenlake and about the general mood in the town, but while he also told him of his own skirmish on Main, he did not give the real reason for it. Instead he observed somewhat wryly: 'You're a dangerous man to know.'

'So,' said Farrer, 'George is actually bringin' a posse out here.'

'That's the word I have,' said Garrick, 'an' it's my bet he'll rope in Dave Dehl an' maybe half a dozen more from down at Hesse's, though he could have a little trouble flushing some of 'em out of there. Then there's the C Star herd. I'd say Clayburgh's sent word by now for some hands to help fetch it out of your canyon, so maybe Clayburgh won't ride with George. It's hard to say.'

'When I move I'll do it real careful.'

'Move where to?'

'Just far enough to keep out o' their

sights,' Farrer said, 'an' keep tryin' to turn up somethin' — or somebody — to tell me who in hell it was that moved those animals an' why they were kept there.'

'You can't dodge around an' wait 'em out forever,' said Garrick.

'What the hell else can I do?'

'Try trusting Wenlake.'

Farrer gave a short, bitter laugh. 'Oh, I don't altogether mistrust George, but what's he goin' to do, faced with the fact of the C Star beef on my range, in numbers, hidden away?'

Garrick had to accept that what Farrer was saying was all too logical and he could not readily come up with options, so he took another tack. 'Everything points to them being taken in there in bunches, the last one the biggest, exactly what Clayburgh's been saying all along; but left there by who an' for how long?'

'They were in there to be all driven out later,' said Farrer, 'probably at night; but it's not a good place to leave

84

animals for long, no feed an' no water.'

'Driven out who by? The same people that took 'em in, or others?'

Farrer thought that others were involved and recounted the story that Smith had brought home with him, of unknown riders on the hills inside the Flying F line. 'Maybe they were the ones who had come in to move the herd, then backed off when Smith got too close to them, an' made to get closer.'

Garrick said: 'Let's say that, whoever they were, they were from outside Blayrock County, come to move more than two hundred head, cattle that had seen money change hands, cattle that now they won't get their ropes on.'

'Unless they've already got 'em on the move,' Farrer said, and smiled. 'Which would be the best thing as far as I'm concerned. I could hardly move 'em all on my own, so if they've gone, it might put me in the clear.'

'Unless George uses the same reasoning we've just used,' said Garrick. 'I wouldn't put any money on getting in the clear that easy. What I think will happen is that Clayburgh will get in without any delay an' get his cows back onto C Star. Dan would see it as first things first, now that George will be on the job, expected to fetch in the guilty man before too much longer. So think about this: if any money's changed hands over this herd, but Clayburgh recovers the herd, what'll the next move likely be?'

'They'll want their coin back, who-ever they are; or before too much longer, they'll want another two hundred head or more.' Then Farrer shrugged. 'This is a hell of a lot of guesswork, Wes.'

'Yeah, I know it. But it's the best hope we've got. An' there's another thing, provided Wenlake's posse doesn't run you to ground inside a couple of days, the kind of scum that he'll have raked together is going to lose heart for it an' start tellin' him. It'll turn out to be real thirsty work so they'll want to get it over an' done with real quick. An' once they're off your range, maybe we won't have too long to wait before some more of Clayburgh's stock gets a night drive.' He shot a quick look at Farrer. 'But whatever happens, we can't afford to take Dave Dehl cheap, or that Hagan bastard. They could easy keep their eye on the ranch, with or without George knowing it.'

The concern showed at once in Farrer's face, for this was something that had never been far from his own thoughts. 'Liz.'

Garrick said: 'Hagan's the one I'd worry about most.'

'I'll kill any of the scum that goes anywhere near her,' Farrer said. He walked away a few paces and gave careful scrutiny to the brushlands all around them. Finally he was satisfied that there was no dust from incoming riders and came walking back towards Garrick who was standing rubbing the long nose of the black horse. It was then that in a low voice Farrer told Garrick of the strains, the tensions that had arisen between him and Liz. 'I don't know why, Wes. I don't even know if there is a particular *why* or whether it's just somethin' that's grown, over the years. Maybe she's sick an' tired of this damn life out here, for it's sure as hell not been easy; an' now there's more problems than ever over money. Maybe she's started askin' herself why, after all the struggles we've had, all the effort we've both put in, we still seem to be slidin' backwards. It's been a damn' treadmill that's never showed any signs of stoppin'.'

'You've not talked with her about it?'

Farrer spread his hands in a gesture of hopelessness, then let them fall to his sides again. 'I've tried, Wes — or I used to try, but gave it up when I didn't seem to be gettin' anywhere. Liz, well, she don't seem to *want* to talk. She's kind of . . . drawn away. When that happens, after a while there don't seem to be any more you can do.'

'I'm sorry,' said Garrick. He could see

no profit in saying that rumours had already spread out through the county and that people were providing their own theories.

'Which doesn't mean I've come to think any less of her,' said Farrer. 'If anything had to happen to her . . . ' He looked at Garrick squarely. 'Will you go see her Wes? Will you do your best to keep an eye on her 'til this dies down? I know it's a lot to be askin', but . . . '

'I'd planned to go there first off,' Garrick said, 'to make sure she was all right, find out if she'd heard from you. Then I got hold of the idea you might've come to this place, close to C Star range, where they wouldn't expect you to be.' After a moment, he said: 'I'll go see Liz.' The words were flat, without emotion, giving away nothing of his personal dilemma, of his problems with Emily, or of his own thoughts of Liz herself. This was not the time, if indeed there was a time. He said then: 'You plan to move from here, now?'

Farrer nodded. 'Yeah. I might even go

as far as Benning Forks for a day or so, an' hope they've not yet got the word. I'll need some supplies.'

'That's a damn' big risk to take,' said Garrick. 'You'd be a lot better off lying low somewhere, keeping a good look out for Wenlake, an' wait for me to get some supplies out to you from the ranch.'

'Don't get yourself in bad trouble over me, Wes.'

'I don't like Dave Dehl an' some of the others that George is bound to have with him, an' I have an advantage over George; I know that it has to be somebody else that rustled Clayburgh's damn' stock. I'll take my chances. Now the best thing we can do is work out somewhere safe where you can hole up an' wait for me to fetch the supplies out.'

Farrer thought about it for a short time and then he said: 'I can't say it enough; you'll need to go real careful Wes.' And because Garrick had not chosen to tell him what it was that had happened, to leave him with visible injuries, Farrer made a small gesture with his hand. 'To me it don't look like you've been careful enough.'

Garrick smiled bleakly. 'Hagan. Then for good measure, Dehl an' Ryder. George Wenlake stopped it before it got to the stage where my arms got torn off. So I'm more than a little in this already, Jim.'

Farrer shook his head slowly, looking weary and even, for the first time, dispirited. Then, intuitively perhaps: 'What does Emily have to say about it?'

'I think George has been busy working on Emily, but that started a long while before all this blew up, for other reasons, all of them to do with George.' He turned away and swung up into the saddle, having said more than he had intended. 'Best get moving. There's a lot to be done.'

They then agreed that Garrick would now go straight to the Flying F, and some time after sundown would head on out again, riding due west from the ranch-house, carrying whatever supplies he could, and somewhere between there and a place that Garrick also knew, called Barber's Ridge, Farrer would be waiting for him.

'Don't look for me,' said Farrer, 'I'll watch an' listen for you.'

'By the time I get to you it could be near to midnight,' Garrick said.

A little after supper-time, Garrick was at Flying F. Liz, her face in the lamplight looking strained, came onto the porch and she stopped short when she saw who it was. 'Oh . . . Wes. I thought . . . '

'It was Jim?'

'Yes.'

'Well, I've seen him an' he's all right.'

She insisted on making supper for him and she had Smith take the black horse to be watered and fed. When, later, Garrick was sitting back sipping coffee, she sat down opposite him to listen while he told her of his run-in with C Star in Blayrock, to his arrangement with Farrer, and he spoke about Wenlake and the posse which, they must now assume, he had now formed and which might be camped somewhere out on the range. When he said that was all he could tell her she sat looking at him for what seemed a long time, her grey eyes unmoving, and then she said: 'And what about Emily, Wes? You haven't once mentioned Emily.'

'Emily's still fetching an' carrying an' generally running after George. An' listening to George.'

'Have you quarrelled?'

He shrugged. 'If it was a quarrel then it was part of the same one we've been having for some good while; about George, an' not about Clayburgh's damn' cattle.'

The large grey eyes continued to study him, and so searchingly that he felt that they were actually exposing his unexpressed thoughts. Then in a quiet but neutral tone she said: 'That's something you'll need to work out and deal with soon, Wes, or not at all.'

He found he had looked away from

the calm, direct gaze, discomfited by it, perhaps, and stood up. 'The sooner I can get the provisions out to Jim, the sooner he can get right out of sight for a time.'

'Where will he go?'

'He'll be keeping on the move as much as he can. We don't believe the kind of posse that George is likely to form, will have a lot of staying power.'

Liz stood up and moved away to begin getting the supplies ready, but while she was doing it she kept glancing at Garrick, probing for his views as she voiced an opinion that had a very familiar sound.

'He can't just stay out of sight forever, Wes. They already have what they see as evidence, and whatever might happen with this posse, Wenlake won't let up until Jim's been taken.'

'We've talked about that,' Garrick said. 'With any luck, if he can keep out of their way for a few days, maybe a week, then that first search will probably peter out, then — '

She broke in: 'What good will that do? There'll be others. Maybe they'll even bring marshals in.'

Garrick nodded, aware of her sharp concern. 'I know, but one thing we do have on our side, an' that's the fact of human greed; an' maybe one or two other things. We have to hope that something comes up to put a doubt in George Wenlake's mind.'

'But we don't have any right to bring you into this,' she said.

'I'm in it because I want to be in it,' Garrick told her, then looked seriously at her. 'You keep a rifle handy here in the house, Liz, 'til this is over. Don't trust *anybody* apart from young Smith out there. You understand me?'

She nodded and turned towards him. Soft fingers touched his arm, his battered face, even as Emily's had done. 'Be careful, Wes, I — we don't want you harmed any more.'

7

It was approaching three o'clock in the morning by the time Garrick, under the light of a pale moon, again came within sight of the Flying F ranch-house. He had taken a sackful of provisions, a bedroll and blankets out as far as Barber's Ridge and had waited there, and when Farrer had assured himself that the lone horseman was indeed Garrick, he had come to him, riding out of the gloom.

Now Garrick's eyes were burning and his head was feeling heavy from fatigue as he walked the black horse through the ranch yard towards the barn, from where, as soon as he had unsaddled the animal, he intended to make his way to the bunkhouse and there, without disturbing Smith, sleep for a few hours.

Hardly had he lifted the saddle off the horse, however, than a lamp glowed yellowly in the ranch-house and then he saw the small, light-robed figure of Liz Farrer come out on the porch. Garrick made sure that there was feed available for the black, and water, then stroked the animal's sleek neck before walking outside and across the yard to the porch.

'He came to me,' Garrick said. 'Within ten minutes of me reaching Barber's he was heading away into the broken country up beyond there. Now the cat an' mouse begins.'

With folded, enclosing arms she drew her light-coloured robe around her. 'I've got a bed made up for you.' Before he could even think of anything to say, she had turned away and gone inside. Garrick went up the steps.

A bed had indeed been made up in a curtained annex off the kitchen. Garrick was concerned that he would sleep beyond the four hours that he would allow himself, for he must return to Blayrock as soon as possible to take a wagon to Benning Forks, there to pick up freight that would be waiting at the railroad depot.

'I'll be sure to wake you,' Liz promised, 'and you'll have a meal before you set out.'

She was as good as her word, for he awoke after four hours to gentle but persistent shaking and to the appetizing smell of breakfast sizzling in kitchen pans. By the time he had risen and washed and finished dressing, though still affected by lack of sleep, the meal was being put on the table for him, Liz then moving around the kitchen attending to numerous tasks as though obeying some self-imposed compulsion to keep busy. She was wearing a plain and simple house dress which, ordinary though it was, could do nothing to defeat the impression she gave of slimness and small roundness, her dark hair pulled back and piled at the nape of her neck, secured with a scrap of yellow ribbon. It was impossible for him — as it would have been for any man — not to be disturbingly aware of her physical presence; and he gained the distinct impression that she well knew it. Presently her grey eyes turned towards him and she asked:

'Will you be coming back?'

He sipped rich coffee, then nodded. 'Tomorrow though, I have to take a wagon up to the Forks, an' I've got other things that have to be done, or laid out for Lem Alford to do. Elder's due back in Blayrock tomorrow, before noon; but yeah, I told Jim I'd be around here in about four days from now. By that time he's maybe going to need some more supplies.'

'If he intends being on the move, how will you find him?'

'There's a particular valley that both of us know, in the foothills of the Chaters. He'll wait there an' be on the look-out for me; on the look-out for anybody else, as well.'

'There's a whole lot of risk in all this, Wes, for you as much as for Jim.'

'Like I told you last night Liz, I'm in it because I want to be, an' for a whole bunch of reasons.'

Her dark head had bowed and it was a second or two before he realized that there were tears, and even as he stood up, she crossed the room quickly and clung to him, her small body trembling, her sobbing audible but muffled against his chest. Then at last she straightened up and stood a little away from him, groping for a handkerchief for her tear-wet face, and shaking her head as though in utter confusion and dismay.

'Wes, I'm sorry. I — it's been a bad few hours here, coming right on top of a lot of other things. We've got no right to involve you, no matter what you say. You've done more than enough as it is, and you've been hurt already on account of it.' She drew in a shaking breath, trying to smile at him.

'We'll all get through this somehow Liz,' said Garrick. 'The one solid fact we have is that Jim didn't do what they say he did, so somebody else in this county must reckon they're free an' clear. There's all different kinds of people around here, like anywhere, an' that's something we can maybe get to use before long. Don't lose heart, Liz. An' do be careful.'

This time she did manage to smile, pointing to a corner of the room where leaned a rifle that belonged to Farrer. 'I haven't forgotten what you said to me. And I can rely on Smith, young as he is.'

Garrick did not draw as much comfort from that as Liz apparently did but he held back from saying so, for he had no wish to unsettle her further. 'Time I got on my way.'

'Finish your coffee. I'll go out and have Smith get the horse saddled and brought out of the barn.' She left him and he could hear her calling for the ranch-hand as she went across the yard.

There was a sweet scent to her that lingered faintly from when she had clung to him and he could still almost feel the soft litheness of her body, leaving him with a sensation almost of guilt, even though there still remained between them, as there had been all along, a line uncrossed, and even though he had made no move towards her. Yet it was impossible, just through being in the same room with her, not to become deeply aware of her soft sensuality, and it was an effort for him to put to one side recurring thoughts of her. The coffee was still unfinished and several quiet minutes had passed before he walked out onto the porch, even as the body of horsemen arrived in the yard, lifting dust, the horses themselves blowing and stepping and screwing sideways, heads tossing, metal clinking. Wenlake and his posse.

They did not immediately see Garrick for their attention was first on Smith who had just come leading the saddled black out of the barn, then on Liz. With Wenlake were six men, three from Blayrock whom Garrick knew only by sight as frequenters of Hesse's, Dave Dehl, the tall, cast-eyed man and the hulking Ryder. There was no sign of either Hagan or Clayburgh himself.

Wenlake was saying something to Liz,

something patterned, about not wishing to alarm her but that he had a clear duty to perform and that he had here with him a lawful posse, sworn for the purpose of bringing in, alive, her husband, James Farrer, to answer to charges of rustling more than two hundred head of prime beef, the property of Daniel Clayburgh. What Liz might have said to all of that was never to be known for it was then that Ryder, leaning across, said something to Wenlake and they all turned their heads to look at Garrick who was now coming down the steps off the porch. Wenlake's jaw dropped and then, a flush invading his sharp face, he said:

'Well, now, what have we here? Ain't you a mile or two out o'your way, Garrick?'

Garrick went walking easily across the dry, hot yard and stopped about ten feet in front of the horsemen.

'I come an' go as I please anywhere around this county,' he said.

Dehl let out a short, harsh laugh. 'Do

we get to guess why yuh picked this here place right now mister?' He shot a sidelong glance towards Liz, one which required no further interpretation, and indeed at once gave rise to a ripple of chuckling through the posse.

'When women in remote places get left alone, an' through none of their own doing,' Garrick said, 'it's always a matter of interest to see how long it takes the county scum to show up. Where friends are concerned, I like to keep an eye on that.'

Dehl, his anger manifest, made as though to get down out of the saddle but Wenlake reached across quickly and grabbed at his elbow.

'Hold up there, Dave. This ain't the rooster we've come here for.'

Dehl continued to stare hard at Garrick but finally rebuked. 'Oh, yuh'll keep, wagon-man.'

To Liz Farrer, Wenlake said: 'That man o'yours been back here?'

'No. You can look if you want.' Wenlake turned his head as though to ask Smith perhaps the same question, but Liz, guessing that, cut him off short. 'I've already told you, Mr Wenlake, that my husband hasn't been back here. And small wonder he hasn't.' She nodded towards Dave Dehl. 'If he'd not got out when he did, that night, that man there would have seen him hanging from the hoist-beam. If you want Jim then you'll have to go find him, and I wish you luck, for you'll need plenty, heading a rabble like this. I don't want to see any of these vermin anywhere near my house again, whether you claim them as sworn men or not. I hope that's clear to you, and I'll bid you good-day.'

Wenlake's face was a study and he seemed too taken aback to make an immediate reply. Ryder, however, was quicker off the mark.

'Yuh got a bad mouth there, lady, that could get yuh in real trouble an' then yuh'd be in it along with that cow-thievin' man o'yourn.'

'If you're an example of what now represents the law in this county,' said

Liz, looking unswervingly at Ryder, 'then plainly we're all reaching a long way down in the sack.' And to Wenlake. 'Are these really the best you could get, Mr Wenlake?'

Visibly stung now, probably, Garrick thought, because what she had said was uncomfortably close to the truth, Wenlake said; 'Who I get to help me uphold the law at any time is my business, an' if your man didn't have a real serious charge hangin' over him, Miz Farrer, whether you take us kindly or not, we wouldn't otherwise, not none of us be way out here in this Goddamn' heat, ridin' all over, lookin' for him.' He made an abrupt signal with one gloved hand, and in a flurry of dust, led his party as it went wheeling away and headed out across the Flying F range, southeastward.

So angry had Liz become that she was still trying to get her breathing under control as minutes went by and as the riders diminished, receding into the distance, all spread out now in a long line, maybe eighty to a hundred yards between the horsemen, like a skirmish line, as though their intention was to comb the countryside in that fashion, in the belief that if one rider did not sight the quarry, then another would. Finally, Liz looked somewhat ruefully at Garrick.

'I lost my temper with them, Wes, and I know I shouldn't have done that. In the finish it won't make matters any better and might even make them worse.' She paused. Then: 'Of course, it isn't going to look at all good for you, coming out of my house like that, early in the morning.'

The same thought had occurred to Garrick, but now, principally for her sake, he grinned and shrugged in an attempt to make light of it, and then he said: 'The most important thing right now is that Jim keeps out of their sight for the next few days.' He turned, nodded to Smith who handed him the reins, a quiet and clearly subdued young man, having been but a stunned spectator all through, witnessing an unsuspected, fiery spirit that had suddenly revealed itself in the quiet little wife of his employer. Garrick, leather creaking, swung up into the saddle. 'No sign of Hagan or Clayburgh,' he remarked. 'It's my guess they'll have taken others in to fetch the herd out.' And he did not add, but hoped fervently that if such was the case, that same crew would not, by some unhappy chance, catch sight of Farrer. Smith went away towards the corral and Garrick paused a moment or two longer. Liz, now that the posse had gone on its way and her anger had dissipated, looked very small and vulnerable, the many apprehensions that she had now visible in a face that was tired and drawn with strain. Although she seemed close to another breaking point, Garrick was moved to warn her again.

'For a while it would make sense to keep Smith close by. You saw those two I tangled with, close up, maybe for the first time, Dehl and Ryder; now you know what kind they are. They respect nothing an' nobody, certainly not a woman on her own.' Wearily she nodded. Garrick said: 'There was another man among them, did you notice, with a cast in one eye? A tall, thin man.' He paused. 'I reckon I ought to know who he is, but I just can't bring him to mind; but he bothers me somewhat.' He glanced over his shoulder. The posse had passed entirely from sight somewhere over the rolling range.

Liz said: 'You saw the expression on Wenlake's face. Finding you out here might cause you trouble with Emily, once he's had the chance to talk with her.'

'That's just one more gamble I'll have to take,' he said, but he knew only too well with what alacrity George Wenlake would indeed use that piece of news.

It was not until he was within sight of Blayrock that the recollection of where it was that he had seen the lanky, cast-eyed man before, came to him and when it did it was sufficient for him to draw the black to a halt for a minute or two while he thought about it. It had in fact been seven or eight years earlier. He had hauled a wagon into a town called Dassler where, a little after noon on a bright, hot day, a dispute had broken out in one of the two seedy saloons there, and when gunfire had exploded and a man, hurled backwards by the impact of lead had come bursting out between the batwing doors, he had rolled from the boardwalk onto the street, shot to death. With others, Garrick had been standing across the street when men from the saloon had come out, one man in a clawhammer coat and two others, white-aproned bar-dogs, together with several others who clearly had been customers. Who had fired the shots, Garrick had not discovered until later, when somebody at a freight yard had told him that it had been a real bad bastard by the name of Augie Parr; and later that same day he had seen a mounted man jogging out of Dassler, a long, skinny man wearing a wide-brimmed, dirty grey hat and range clothing, some of it clumsily patched, and a person nearby had muttered: 'That's him there. That's Parr.' Garrick had got but a momentary glimpse of the rider's bony face as he went passing by, not sufficient to mark it indelibly in Garrick's mind. But today, through a swift impression only, a glance, an attitude, and though the clothing worn had been much better kept, it had been sufficient to partially reawaken the memory of that hot day, long ago, in the town of Dassler. He wondered if George Wenlake could have any idea of the kind of man who was riding at his back.

8

The following day, upon Elder's return, Garrick had taken a wagon up to Benning Forks, and not only that, but to Lem Alford's undisguised delight, had taken the boy along. There would be plenty to do once they got there and Garrick was interested to learn how the youngster would be able to cope, and so gauge his fitness for responsibilities that Alford might yet have to take.

Before he left Blayrock Garrick had not visited Emily, nor had she come to see him. He had not been able to make up his mind whether or not his own failure to go talk with her was simply a reluctance to perhaps provoke another argument, even though her father had not yet returned and consequently could not have told her of Garrick's appearance from out of the Flying F ranch-house, with all the unsavoury implications of that. Instead Garrick told himself that he now needed some time to think over a whole lot of things and that maybe the four day Benning Forks roundtrip, with young Alford along and taking the reins for a good part of the journey, would afford him just the right opportunity to do that. Before setting out, however, he had had a quiet word with Elder, asking him to keep his eyes open and in particular to be wary of the cast-eyed man if he should return to Blayrock at any time with Wenlake's posse.

'His name's Augie Parr. I know of at least one man he shot and killed a few years back, in Dassler, that was, an' the talk there at that time was that he was a real hard-nose an' that he'd killed others, in other places.'

'Does George know who he is?' Elder had asked.

'I don't know. I think maybe not. Anyway, if that posse comes back here with or without Jim Farrer, Parr might just decided to move on out of this county. If he does come back here, just make a point of keeping well out of his way.'

Now, four days on, Garrick and Lem Alford could see the town of Blayrock before them once again and it was with somewhat mixed feelings that Garrick eventually walked his team along the main street at the relatively quiet time of an hour after noon, pausing at a number of premises along the way to set down merchandise, boxes, casks, coils of wire, bolts of cloth, hardware. He was greeted at the freight yard by Steve Elder. Alford, tired or not, jumped down at once and moved forward ready to attend to the freely-sweating team. Elder surveyed the large load still stacked on the wagon and began talking about his own imminent movements, no doubt to make the journey on down to the town of Georgeville and beyond. To the suppressed but obvious disappointment of Lem Alford, still nearby, Garrick did not suggest that the youngster accompany Elder, and Elder

114

himself, no doubt to the boy's dismay, did not mention it. It was something that was to come back to Garrick's mind in the future.

A little time later, when immediate matters had been disposed of, Garrick questioned Elder about events in Blayrock during his absence and one or two things now emerged that were both disturbing and puzzling to Garrick; and while he had been in Benning Forks, some other information had come to him which seemed to inject more doubts into his mind, so for the time being he was keeping it to himself.

Elder, arms folded, was propped against the frame of the yard door as Garrick was finishing a meal and then pushing the plate aside.

'Oh yeah, they're all back in Blay-rock,' Elder said, 'an' I can tell you old George Wenlake wasn't lookin' none too pleased. I don't know how far it was they'd ridden, but them horses looked to be about as beat as the damn' posse an' that was dead beat an' parched.

They went right on up to Hesse's first thing an' left old George up there by his jail lookin' like he'd lost a dollar an' found a dime.'

'It doesn't surprise me too much,' said Garrick. Privately he felt very pleased that the guesses about the posse that he and Farrer had made seemed to have come true. But he asked: 'When was it they got back?'

'Yesterday, about the middle of the mornin'; Dehl, Ryder an' two or three other no-goods.'

'That thin feller too? Augie Parr?'

Elder thought it over for a moment or two, then shook his head. 'Nope. I happened to pass 'em on Main when they first come in. There was Wenlake an' five others, that's all. Not Parr, I didn't think about him.'

'You're sure about that?'

'Yep, no doubt about it.'

Garrick weighed whether or not to say more to Elder about his own concerns for Liz Farrer but came down in favour of not doing so; but he thought he might not be so reticent should he chance to speak with Wenlake. So he simply chose to say: 'I'm not sorry to hear he didn't come back to Blayrock. We can do without his kind.'

'There was one other thing,' said Elder, 'an' it didn't make no sense to me, no sense at all.'

'What?'

'It was the day they come back. I was along by the back o' Hesse's place. I'd been along at the forge to take note of some things Jack Aubrey needs us to get from the Forks, an' I saw Hesse an' Dave Dehl right in back o' Hesse's, Dave rubbin' his horse down, an' I'll tell you this for no charge Wes, that Hesse, he was sure givin' Dave a hard time over somethin' an' it was all one way.'

'Hesse was? I wouldn't fancy his luck, not with Dave Dehl.'

'That sure is what I would've thought,' Elder agreed. ''Course, I couldn't hear what was bein' said, not nothin', but I can tell you that the eyeglasses man, he was sure waggin' the fat finger under Dave Dehl's nose over somethin', an' whatever the reason he had for doin' it, he sure did mean it. Anyway Dehl, he left town not long after an' they say he'd headed back to C Star.'

Garrick thought it over but admitted to being as mystified as was Elder. They both knew that Dave Dehl was simply not the kind of man to allow himself to be dominated by anybody, let alone the overweight and middle-aged proprietor of some seedy saloon. One thing that did always count in Hesse's favour, however, perhaps even with a hard man like Dehl, was the imposing and ever-threatening presence on his pay-roll, of Ryder. No, there were not many, certainly around Blayrock, who would willingly risk tangling with such a man as Ryder, and Garrick was under no illusions as to just how close he himself had come to doing just that, and would have, but for, of all people, Wenlake.

The recollection of that incident prompted him to speculate what

Wenlake might do now, for the prospect of chousing at least half of his posse out of Hesse's or out of their whores' beds to make another tiring sweep across the rangelands of the Flying F might now be considered reasonably remote; Dehl gone, and the cast-eyed man, the most dangerous one, Parr, apparently moved on. The thoughts of Wenlake bore Garrick on naturally to consider if he ought now to go along to talk seriously with Emily; but for the moment, and for indeterminate reasons, he put the idea aside.

'Clayburgh, he was in Blayrock the day before the posse got in. Maybe he come to find out if they'd got back. He looked in at Hesse's, so I'm told, an' then he rode out again. I heard he'd asked a few people some questions about Bolt — like, if anybody had seen Nate around.' Elder grinned. 'Well, Nate didn't happen to be around here, so I reckon the ol' bastard must've run out of *dinero*.'

'Maybe,' said Garrick. Clayburgh and

Bolt. The brooding rancher, no matter what was happening elsewhere, was evidently as unwilling as ever to let go of the idea that Bolt was in some way involved in thefts of cattle. Whether in part this also meant that there was still a seed of doubt remaining in Clayburgh's mind about Farrer, or whether he was simply regarding Bolt as a likely accomplice, Garrick would dearly have liked to know. For now, however, it was simply another teasing thought to turn over in his mind.

Then, coming back to the business at hand, Elder asked: 'You gonna put the boy on one o' the wagons?'

'It might get to a point where I have to,' Garrick said. 'At the Forks an' on the haul back here he proved to me he could handle it. He's smart an' he's a lot stronger than he looks. But if . . . if I'm not around, have him do the Georgeville run. You handle the main haul from the Forks. Anyway, it might not come to that. But I've made promises I've got to keep, which means

I've got to go back out on the Flying F, so for now, Alford stays put right here, an' you do this haul to Georgeville. Likely I'll be back here before you.' By now there were a host of questions, all unconnected with mundane freighting that Elder wanted to ask, but none were invited, and finally Elder, knowing that the moment had passed, nodded, propped off the door-frame and went across the yard to where Garrick could hear Alford turning out the fresh team.

Whether or not at this particular time Garrick wished to talk with George Wenlake, in the event he was left with no choice for just as he was coming along Main, having been up to the general store to garner more business, the Blayrock peace officer, emerging from his office, almost collided with him.

'Ah,' said Wenlake, his sharp-featured face showing no enthusiasm, 'so you're back.'

'It looks like we're all back,' Garrick

said mildly, 'or that's what I hear; all back bar one.'

'You don't waste much time gettin' your long nose to the ground,' Wenlake observed.

'Do you think you'll ever get any of those roosters out of Hesse's for a second go at it?'

Obviously it was a sore point with Wenlake and his sour mien confirmed what Elder had been saying to Garrick about the peace officer's mood when they had all ridden back to town. His face darkening, Wenlake said sharply: 'Whether I do or I don't ain't important no more. I got some other good irons in that fire already, an' if I was you, Garrick, I'd look well to my own affairs from here on. An' maybe you ought to give some serious thought to where you get to — '

Garrick cut in quickly. 'George, you'd be real wise to say no more. Where I go an' when I go an' who I see is my business. If I'm reading you right, you're treading along a real thin line; an' as far as Jim Farrer goes, he's been accused, but there's no proof.'

'Then you tell me why it was he lit out like that if he's a man that's got nothin' to hide. Why ain't he come in?'

'George, we've been all through this before. When Clayburgh got to him, Farrer was as good as on the end of a rope, an' you know that as well as I do.'

'The boy's word; that Smith. His woman's word,' said Wenlake. 'What would you expect her to say?'

'To me, Liz Farrer's word betters any other that's going the rounds of the county.'

'Now, that I can believe,' Wenlake said, too quickly.

At that moment Garrick came very near to losing his temper with the man, but with an immense effort, overcame the temptation and changed tack completely. 'Where's Parr got to?'

Wenlake, having scored his point, had been about to go on by, but now pulled up abruptly. 'How the hell do you know Parr?'

'I don't. I just know who he is.'

Wenlake regarded Garrick narrowly, perhaps, in the circumstances, not wanting to put himself in the position of seeking information from Garrick, said: 'Well, whatever you might think you can do as far as defendin' your great friends, the Farrers goes, you're goin' to have to think again. You were part right about that dead-beat posse, Garrick, I'll give you that; but I'll not need to drag them fellers out of Hesse's nor anywhere else. It does so happen that Parr's got some friends that he claims will leave the likes of this Blayrock bunch in their dust. If he's as good as his word — an' he talks up real strong — then in less'n a week we'll have your Mister James Farrer safely cooped up inside this place.' He moved his head, indicating the Blayrock jail.

As Wenlake had been talking, near to boasting, Garrick's stomach had tightened. What was about to take place, as far as the posse was concerned, changed the odds markedly against Farrer, and without doubt, could put Garrick himself at considerable risk; and anybody else who was close to Jim Farrer. Staring now at the overtly smug expression on George Wenlake's face, Garrick received the distinct impression that the peace officer had no idea at all of Augie Parr's unsavoury history. If he had, surely he would not even contemplate taking him on in this way. Hollowly, Garrick now began to wonder what breed of scum these associates of Parr's might turn out to be. He thought it was just as well that he intended meeting Farrer again, and soon, for the rancher had to be told as soon as possible of the hard men who, it seemed, would soon be scouring his own range for him. It had all gone too far. Garrick made up his mind that, somehow, Wenlake must be compelled to realize just who it was that he was about to put his trust in. At that moment, however, from inside the dimness of the jail office, having come along the passageway from the living quarters, towards the men's voices, Emily, not loudly but quite clearly, said: 'Wes. Please, I'd like a word.'

Wenlake actually chuckled as this time he did move on, leaving Garrick with all of the things about Parr unsaid.

It was perfectly clear right from the start that Wenlake had lost no time in passing on to Emily what he had seen, and no doubt all that he had assumed, while out at the Flying F ranch-house, and again, without any doubt, had put the worst possible construction on it.

'I don't really believe there's much that can be said, but what there is has to be got out of the way now, Wes, so there can never be any misunderstanding about it. I take it you don't want to deny that you did stay there? I mean, in her house?'

'I don't deny it,' Garrick said.

'But if the posse hadn't happened to arrive there when it did, then of course no one would have been any the wiser.'

'Is that what *you* believe?'

She did not answer that question

directly. 'Wes, you've always been
. . . close to her.'

'To them. Close to the both of them.
They've been my friends for a long
while. There've been times when I
needed them. Now they need me.'

'By all accounts, they've not been
friends with one another for some
while.'

Although he knew this to be true he
did not wish to hand her what she
would read as further evidence. 'It's
town gossip. I'd thought better of you
than that, Em.'

'*You'd thought better of me?*' Her
face was flushed with anger now, all of
her disillusionment and anguish beginning to come to the surface, her blue
eyes glistening with tears that could no
longer be held back. When she could
speak again, she said: 'I doubt there's
any more we can talk about, you and I.
Maybe it's just as well that it's come
onto the open now. Later, it would have
been unbearable.'

'I'm not even going to get a chance to

say my piece, then?'

'Wes, do you think there's any more that could be said that would be of earthly use, after what's now happened?'

Suddenly Garrick was angry too, though more at Wenlake than at Emily. Garrick was tense, too, and achingly tired, and very concerned now that he had heard that Augie Parr was about to take a bigger hand in the hunting down of Jim Farrer. Since hearing that, Garrick had had a growing belief that Farrer, if the next posse did succeed in running him to earth, would by some means never make it back into Blayrock. All that Garrick wondered, in fact, was how they would manage to square such a thing with Wenlake. Nonetheless, in spite of what she had said to him, he was about to make a last effort to give Emily his own explanation, for he had nothing to hide; but he did not get an opportunity, for even as he started to speak, she made a gesture of dismissal. 'You've told me all I need to know, Wes. You were out there, and you were with her.' She turned and fled along the passageway, and now, he knew, the real tears were starting to come.

His first impulse was to go after her but at another sound, he too, turned, to see Wenlake standing in the doorway.

'She ain't got no more to say to you, Garrick, that's plain enough.'

Garrick gave the Blayrock peace officer the bleakest of looks as he pushed on by him and out onto the boardwalk, and for the second time in no more than ten minutes, he knew he had come close to striking the man.

9

They were out near one of the two large corrals, horses moving lazily around behind them, Dave Dehl and Clayburgh. What they were now calling, out of odd habit, the Farrer herd, was safely back on the C Star range, but Clayburgh, far from being satisfied, was — as was his nature — ill-tempered and still suspicious and continuing to voice his deep disquiet because the man who had stolen his stock and so very nearly got away with it, was still riding free. Dehl, recognizing all of the signs, had prudently stopped short of defending anyone's part in the recent fruitless search for Farrer, but he did say: 'It was a good, wide sweep we done, all strung out loose. We sure did cover some territory an' we started out from the ranch-house just to be sure he hadn't gone back there. The only thing we come across that we didn't expect, out there, was seein' that mouthy freighter, Garrick. Bold as brass, he come out o' the house; an' I reckon he'd been there with the woman since the day before. I'll tell yuh Dan, that sure did make Wenlake's eyes pop.'

Clayburgh, baggy-eyed, discontented, shoved his sweat-stained hat back and stood, hands on hips, staring at the horses in the corral but really not seeing them.

'We might just have to go in an' kick that Garrick's ass real hard before we've done,' he said. Then he refocused on Dehl. 'We might need to kick some asses all 'round, yet. Believe me, I won't see this Farrer thing dropped. I want that bastard took, so everybody in this Goddamn' county knows it's been done, knows I don't let go. If that ain't done, next thing we know, every little shit that's short of a dollar is gonna be tempted to run off a few head here an' a few head there an' we're right back to where we started.'

'I know it,' Dehl said, 'an' George Wenlake knows it.'

'Wenlake . . . ' Clayburgh rubbed at his stubbly jaw, looked speculatively at the cloud-torn sky that had for the moment drawn a thin veil over the burning sun. 'Sometimes I don't know what the hell to make of George Wenlake. What do yuh know about this next posse o' his? An' who's this rooster Parr?'

'Well, I do know George was no way satisfied with the first bunch,' said Dehl, 'an' Parr, he's about to fetch in one or two boys from down near Georgeville that will take it real serious, or so he claims; an' when he gets 'em up to Blayrock an' Wenlake looks 'em over, Parr reckons Farrer will be as good as in the cage.' He inflated his cheeks. 'Parr? A real hard boy, I'd say. He talks kinda easy most o' the time, but he don't take no shit from nobody.'

Clayburgh was nodding slowly, scratching again at his jaw. 'Just so long as they come up with Farrer, that's all I want. But they'll be lookin' to be paid, Parr an' these others.'

'That'll be George Wenlake's problem,' said Dehl. 'He has to have help from somewhere.' Then: 'Look, Dan, I think the same as you, whatever Wenlake or Parr or any other bastard says. We got to be sure they do get out there after this cow thief an' stick there in the saddles 'til they do nail him. This here outfit ought to have a hand in it to keep 'em all honest, or next thing we know is that Farrer is out o' this county or even out o' the territory.'

Clayburgh thought it over, lips pursed, divided, as Dehl knew he would be, between agreeing to an appealing and no doubt sound proposal, and what he perceived to be the immediate day-to-day needs of his ranch. When, through the long hesitation it seemed that regular tasks needing to be done on C Star might have to prevail, Dehl said:

'There's one other thing that I ain't settled in my mind about, Dan.'

'What's that?'

'Bolt,' Dehl said. 'Bolt an' all this money he seems to have. An' now he's gone from Blayrock an' nobody's sure where he's at. The word is that he ain't gone back on that two-bit spread he's got out there. Now, when Farrer moved them cows o' yours he didn't do it all on his own.' This was the kind of theory which was bound to be well received by Clayburgh, for he still nursed deep suspicions of Nathan Bolt. Eyes narrowed, he nodded slowly.

'Bolt. Yeah.'

'He could even be out there feedin' that Farrer bastard an' not only with chow, but with good word, like where the posse might be, all that an' more. Maybe,' Dehl added, 'maybe when Farrer does get took, there's gonna be two birds found in the trap.'

Again Clayburgh nodded, raking stubby fingers slowly across his stomach. Then, his mind made up, he said: 'Yeah, it makes a lot o' sense. Yuh'd best put a rope on a fresh mount an' go bump knees with Wenlake, an' like yuh say, keep all them buzzards honest.'

★   ★   ★

This time, late in the piece, Garrick changed the plan, but with her agreement, and put all his faith in the young ranch-hand, Smith, who would take more provisions out to Jim Farrer at the agreed meeting place; and as Liz stood at his elbow, Garrick explained carefully to Smith the exact whereabouts of the valley where he assured him Farrer would be waiting. 'He'll be there 'til sundown tomorrow, so you'll need to push on an' get it done an' then get back here *pronto* an' out of the way. George Wenlake's about to form this other posse. Now, chances are he won't have got that done yet, but for the sake of your own hide as well as Farrer's, you have to believe they're out already, so don't take even half a chance of leading anybody to Jim. Wenlake's next bunch will be a lot different from the first lot

135

he had, so make sure you tell Jim that, an' tell him there's a man called Augie Parr who'll be with 'em, a tall, skinny *hombre* with a cast eye, an' he'd best not get close enough to see that. There'll be others, brought in by this Parr that I don't know, but like sticks to like, so Jim had best watch how he goes. If he wants to know where I got all this from, about Parr, tell him it was direct from George Wenlake.'

Smith nodded, wanting to do well, in particular for the sake of the worried woman standing listening to this, but he looked anxious, even somewhat fearful, which could be no bad thing as far as personal survival and Farrer's safety was concerned.

So Smith finally departed and it was then that Garrick saw very clearly on her face the immense strain that Liz was living under. The deep anxieties of past days had accumulated until now there was about her an unfamiliar deadness, a lack of spirit, as though, watching Smith riding away, and having heard in taut silence all that Garrick had had to say to him, she too had come to recognize fully and probably for the first time, the kind of adversaries now about to confront them. She said to Garrick:

'This man Parr, maybe because I was confused and off balance, I don't exactly remember him when he came here before with Wenlake. But he really is a different sort of man, isn't he?'

Garrick thought there could be no point in trying to make it seem otherwise. 'Yes. It's now going beyond the kind of men we think about around Blayrock as hard-noses. I'm sure Wenlake doesn't know what he's got hold of. I set out to tell the man, but George is stubborn an' once he takes a set against somebody he's real hard to shift. He sees only his own grudge. So I was the wrong man to be trying to tell George anything. I'd have done it though, because I thought it was important enough, but Emily came along an' broke in on us. After that, I guess I lost heart.'

'Emily.' Liz Farrer repeated the name as though she had only just recalled it, but knowing that as far as Garrick was concerned it was not simply a matter of whether or not he was in George Wenlake's favour, it was Wenlake's daughter who would be more important to him.

'It's all got out of hand,' said Garrick.

'Because of . . . ' She had actually started to say *because of me*, but checked, and said: 'Because of us, Jim and me.' It was not a question but a statement.

'Because of me making up my own mind to offer some help to some long-time friends.'

Liz shook her head, her grey eyes serious, now prepared to admit only truths. 'You don't have to dress it up for me, Wes, for though I'm sometimes foolish, I'm not a fool. Often, between women, a single glance is all it takes; and for long enough I've been able to read what it is that Emily really believes. She thinks there's a lot more between you and me than friendship.' So it was out now, and in a sense Garrick was glad of it. 'That was it, really, wasn't it?'

There was no point in his trying to avoid the issue, so after a moment he nodded. 'She wouldn't listen to anything I had to say. She'd already made her mind up. In some ways I don't blame her. George was the one who carried the tale and made it sound the way he wanted it to sound; the way I believe he's always wanted it to be.'

Liz looked down briefly. Then: 'If I'd not made up a bed for you in the house . . . '

He shook his head dismissively, and as much to ease her feelings as anything else, said: 'George would have made it look bad no matter what.' He could see though that all this on top of the anguish she must now be feeling, knowing of the very real prospect that her husband would be run down now that a more determined body of hunters would be out sweeping the range for him, had taken its toll of her resources.

'It's hopeless, Wes. Sometimes I've thought he might just as well go in and give himself up. At least Wenlake has the authority in this county.'

Garrick's own unexpressed fears about how effective, in the end, Wenlake might prove to be, he had not the heart to reveal to her, for it was a morbid speculation whose only effect, he thought, would have been to increase her distress. And distress it truly was, for she was now in tears and reaching for him, and suddenly for the second time in recent hours was clinging to him as though he might well represent the only solace she might find in a world that seemed suddenly to have turned all of its malevolence upon her. He did his best to soothe her, an unaccustomed, awkward role for Garrick, and then persuaded her to go inside and sit down, and when she did, he knelt near her until gradually she got herself under control. Presently, in a low but steadier voice, she returned to this idea of Farrer actually giving himself up; but now she modified that view when she told Garrick she believed that Jim, at the outset, would have been best advised to get right out of the county for a time, until she herself could have gone into Blayrock and attempted to persuade Wenlake to abandon any idea of a posse, to settle the more excitable folk down, and allowed her to negotiate a meeting between Jim and Wenlake himself. Again Garrick pondered this implied, implicit belief in the solidity of Wenlake, for personally he felt that it was a highly dangerous line to be taking, no matter what greater risks Farrer might have to face in trying to out-fox this next posse; and it was perfectly possible that Farrer, the accused cow thief, might first be sighted by some passing rider who, observing his line-of-ride, could in short order bring Wenlake and his men down on him. That was a danger that from now on would stalk Farrer constantly. In the brooding silence which now fell between them Garrick felt inadequate in that he could offer this beleaguered woman no honestly grounded hope, except that he, free to move whenever and wherever he chose, might yet discover something in Farrer's favour sufficient to make Wenlake listen to him.

It was not until he had long departed from the Flying F, however, and indeed had again come within sight of Blayrock, that he faced the conclusion that, if he were to be honest, had never been far away from his mind ever since the beginning of this bad affair; that was, that if anything of value were to be discovered, then he, Garrick, could not afford simply to wait for it to appear. He must make some move to make it happen; and if he did that, then the die was indeed cast, and he might quite easily find himself out on his own, exposed, and virtually isolated among men who could be very dangerous indeed. Nonetheless, long before he finally rode into his own freight yard he had made up his mind what he would do, and that was to play an instinct, following up something that he had learned in conversation with Elder, and in so doing, would choose to take that extreme risk.

When he did arrive in Blayrock, however, the first person he saw there was George Wenlake himself, striding along the boardwalk towards the jail and certainly looking none too pleased. Perhaps because matters had not been going his way in recent hours, the peace officer came to a stop when he saw who it was walking the black horse onto Main and said:

'So, you been out there again? Been offerin' some more warm comfort to the poor deserted wife I've no doubt. Any sign o' that bastard Farrer?' When Garrick drew the horse to a halt and did not offer an immediate answer, merely holding his anger in check, Wenlake went on: 'Listen, if I ever find out you been givin' any help to that feller — an' make no mistake, it'll all come out in the finish — I'll have you inside that cage in there right along with him.'

Garrick chose not to make the

righteous denial that no doubt was expected of him, but said in a level voice: 'Something gone wrong here George? What is it? Your hard men failed to show up?'

'Oh they'll be here, mister,' Wenlake said, reddening though, 'an' it might just pay you to keep well clear of 'em when they do get in.'

Garrick knew that here was the opportunity to drive home what he now regarded as an important point, and he did it, staring unswervingly at the sharp-faced, irascible man, and in a way that caused Wenlake to reappraise him carefully. 'George, I want you to rein in your tongue for just half a minute an' you can listen and pass this along to whatever scum you finally swear in. What might happen to Farrer is one thing: the welfare of his wife is another. If any of your hired assholes gets ideas an' lifts a finger against Liz Farrer, I'll come after whoever it might be an' I'll send him on to Jehovah with his eyes bulging an' a hole where his belly was.'

The white fury that had been building in Garrick had begun to show in the bleakness of his face, in the chilling certainty behind the look that he was now giving Wenlake; and it got home, that much Garrick knew, for George Wenlake's head moved up and back slightly, almost as though there had been a physical blow to back up Garrick's words. Wenlake said no more but turned on his heel and went inside the jail office, the door slamming behind him.

Garrick moved the horse on. At the corner of the alley that ran down alongside the Blayrock jail he now saw that the slim figure of Emily had paused, a cane basket on her arm, she having apparently been in the act of returning from shops, and having without any doubt overheard all that had passed between Garrick and her father; and now with a flicker of her blue skirts, she too turned her back on the horseman and vanished from his sight.

The first arrival for Wenlake's posse, Dave Dehl, came into Blayrock the next morning, but it was not until that afternoon that Augie Parr and two companions arrived and hitched their horses outside Hesse's. When young Alford came jogging into the yard and told him they had arrived, Garrick, so that he would know them again should he see them, made it his business to get close enough to take a look. What he saw made his stomach tighten and for the first time he really did see what they were now up against.

10

Next morning it seemed that all of Blayrock chose to be in the vicinity to get a good look at George Wenlake's second posse when the men who were to ride in it came ambling out of Wenlake's office and got ready to mount up.

Dave Dehl was there of course, sour as ever, and the lanky Parr with the odd eyes, pacing up and down, one glove on, slapping the other in the palm of a hand. By this time the names of the other two had been passed from mouth to mouth: Les Eardley and Buck Thomas. Eardley was a cat-like slow mover, a medium-sized man, slim hipped, dressed all in sober clothing that was not new but that looked as though particular care had been taken with it; dark pants tucked into black boots, a pale grey shirt with a black leather vest over it, an ink-blue bandanna and a black, shallow, loose-thonged hat with a very wide brim. Eardley, like his companions, was hung about with a thickly-shelled belt and a heavy pistol, the holster tied down to his right thigh, and that part of the weapon that was visible, clearly well oiled, the black steel butt plate sandwiched in plain wood of a deep reddish-brown colour. Eardley had a cigar between his teeth, teeth which, particularly at the top were spaced rather widely apart, and his eyes were black, but they were dead, spiritless eyes, utterly devoid of feeling.

The one known as Buck Thomas was somewhat rougher in appearance than Eardley, of slightly larger build, more muscular, and he wore faded levis and dark blue shirt, and over it a sand-coloured jacket of calfskin, short enough to allow the butt of his heavy pistol to stand out clear from his thigh. The jacket was secured at the front with four studs of dull metal and thus could in no way restrict access to the butt of the gun. Thomas's hat was shallow-crowned like Eardley's but dark grey in colour, and looked as though it had been trampled more than once. Thomas's face was like old leather and his lower lip was noticeably scarred, a whitish line running slantwise, left to right, ending near the jaw-line.

If Wenlake had had even one second thought about these men after he had got a look at them, he showed no evidence of it but followed them outside to the horses and swung up, continuing to look decisive, as the man in charge should, and soon afterwards led all four out of Blayrock, heading, Garrick noted with some concern, not in a direction which would take them out onto rangelands beyond the Flying F ranch-house, but directly towards the foothills of the Chaters. Garrick stood watching until the posse was but a small clump of bobbing blobs, quivering in bars of heat, then made his way back to the freight yard.

Now he must plan what his next move was to be and try to lay up some element of safety in case it went badly wrong. Whatever happened he knew he was about to start something which could blow up in his face. Even so, he had no intention whatsoever of going armed, for to do so might well mark him out for the most violent of retribution as well as putting him on the wrong side of the law; and as it was, he would be brushing close enough to that. First, however, he talked seriously with Lem Alford.

'I'm going to be busy for a while. I want you to stay here at the yard an' if anybody comes looking for me, you don't know where I've gone nor when I'll be back, understand?' Though clearly mystified, Alford nodded, and Garrick went on: 'No matter what happens, no matter what you might come to hear, you stay right where you are. Just get on with the usual work, groom the horses, check over all the harness and put any of that aside that looks to be in need of attention.' He knew that Alford's eyes were on him as first he walked away across the yard and into one of the smaller of the outbuildings where spare wagon wheels had been stacked. Garrick looked around, then selected a single wagon-spoke, hefted it in one hand, balanced it, the muscles in his strong forearm roping thickly.

When he left the yard, Alford now no longer in view, he did not do so by the main entrance but walked out onto the back street that ran parallel to Main. Even now his intentions were not formed in detail, but he had seized upon one thing which, if his surmise was anywhere near correct, might be used in some way to relieve at least part of the weight being put on Jim Farrer. This stemmed from Elder's story of pressure of some strange kind being exerted on Dave Dehl by the tubby saloon-keeper, Hesse. Dehl had been prominent in Wenlake's first posse and at various times had been loud in his suspicions of

Nathan Bolt and where Bolt might be getting his ready money from. If there was in turn something vulnerable to be discovered about Dehl himself, then Garrick was determined to find out what it was and maybe give the C Star foreman something else to think about, and so divert his attention, at least for a time, from Farrer. Dehl had gone out in the second posse, too, the only man from the first posse apart from Wenlake, to do so, and his time away from the ranch would be costing Clayburgh something; and Clayburgh was a man well known for counting his coin carefully and to put the immediate needs of his C Star before all else. So Garrick had speculated, too, upon whose idea it might have been for Dehl to go out again and be absent perhaps for some while. In Garrick's mind it had added up to a suspicion, albeit a tenuous one, involving Hesse and Dehl, and was coupled with what he already knew about Bolt. But walking now along the back street towards the rear of

Hesse's he also had to ask himself if he was not in fact seeing significance where there was none, and only because he was almost desperate to relieve in any way he could the dreadful situation the Farrers were in; the dreadful state that he had seen Liz Farrer to be in, that had caught at him, put him off balance in a way that earlier he would not have thought even possible. Yet he did not think less of Emily, even though what she had said, unjustly, still stabbed at him. And Emily surely had made her mind perfectly clear to him. So that door had closed, leaving him to contemplate a personal wilderness and had left him with an extraordinary sense of guilt. Perhaps indeed he was a fool. After all, he was not fitted for this. He was a freight hauler, not a fighter, not a risk-taker. Maybe if what he was now about to attempt should all go wrong, and if Wenlake should ever discover that he had indeed helped Farrer directly, it might cost him not only some liberty, but also the freighting business he had worked so long and hard to build up. Yet he had to remind himself, now that Hesse's yard had come into view, that one unassailable fact remained in all of this; someone had run off C Star cattle but whoever it had been, it had not been Jim Farrer.

Hesse's yard was deserted so Garrick moved on through it towards the back of the saloon, an old, sun-warped building with dirt-flecked windows and whose back door was standing wide open. He went up two shallow steps and inside to find that he was in a kitchen which was as empty as the yard had been. There was a door with vari-coloured glass panels in it. He opened it and found himself in a short, musty passageway with a strip of threadbare brown carpet laid along the centre. In here he became aware, too, of the sourish smell of liquor that permeated all of Hesse's, overlaid with the heavily sweet scent of cigar smoke. Doors gave off either side of this passage and there was another door at the far end, also with coloured glass in it.

Garrick opened one of the side doors and saw a room where stood a table and several chairs and some shelving with crockery stacked on it, but the place was unoccupied. The door behind him, opposite, opened, and when he turned, there was Hesse himself, steel-rimmed eyeglasses glinting, in dark pants, white shirt with expander arm bands, a blue string tie and a silver-grey vest with a gold-watch chain looped across it.

'What the hell do yuh think you're up to?' Hesse asked, and as he drew the next breath, probably to yell for Ryder, Garrick moved swiftly, bringing to the fore the brutal-looking wagon-spoke, pushing the thick end of it to within an inch of Hesse's round little mouth.

'Shut it,' Garrick said. 'Move on back real easy.'

Hesse went shuffling backwards, glasses tending to magnify his eyes, mouth now hanging open, and Garrick saw that they were in an office which contained an old desk, a couple of chairs, some wooden cabinets, a steel safe and shelving with papers and folders on it. Garrick quietly closed the door behind him.

'Listen — ' Hesse began again.

'No,' said Garrick over the top of him, 'you listen. One way or another, you've got a rope on Dave Dehl an' I want to know what it's for. Beginning now, you've got five seconds to start telling me.'

Hesse's smooth face which a moment ago had drained of colour now flushed with sudden anger. 'Yuh got no right to come in here callin' the odds, Garrick, so yuh can get out an' mind your own damn' business while your luck still holds.'

'You're not listening,' Garrick said and pushed the end of the wagon-spoke against Hesse's bulging grey vest, causing him to sit down abruptly in one of the chairs. 'Dave Dehl. Is it over money? I won't ask again.' Hesse's eyes flicked towards the door, then back to the menace of the wagon-spoke. He was starting to perspire, his brow shining. Finally he nodded jerkily.

'I hold some o' Dave's notes,' he said, but found enough spirit to add: 'But that's his business an' mine, an' sure ain't none o' yours.'

Garrick prodded him in the chest. 'Get the notes.' When, ashen-faced, Hesse failed to move instantly, Garrick said: 'Let me see 'em now or have your fat little head opened up with this.' His tone was quite flat, dispassionate, and Hesse had come to see that he was dealing with a man who, unexpectedly, would do as he said he would do. Hesse stood up carefully, Garrick stepping back a little, and went to the safe and unlocked it. The bunch of small papers that he handed to Garrick were all made out in purple ink, presumably by Hesse himself, and all had Dehl's clumsy signature at the bottom. The dates spread over quite some time and the amounts varied but Garrick's eyebrows lifted when he calculated what the total was. 'Something of a card man, Dave, an' not such a good one at that.' He handed the papers back to Hesse. 'How the hell would he get that kind of money on what Clayburgh pays?'

'That's his problem, not mine,' said Hesse thickly, then relief flooded into his face, for the door opened and Ryder came in. 'Take the bastard!' Hesse screamed.

Ryder, as was his custom, was wearing no pistol, but he towered over Garrick, his forearms like hams and his wide, cruel face almost impassive as he glanced from Hesse to Garrick who was backing off slightly, the big man between him and the open door. Hesse had not shifted from near the safe and he still had Dehl's notes in one fat hand. Ryder almost smiled in his contempt of the wagon-spoke that Garrick was holding, and took a step forward, big arms reaching out. Garrick, however, did not make the basic error of swinging the spoke sideways but used it end-on, always a more dangerous attack, holding it in both hands, driving the big end into

Ryder's solar plexus, sinking it deep, fetching what was almost a shriek of agony from the ox-like man, causing him to go staggering back a couple of paces, clutching at his middle.

Hesse went lunging towards the desk where, in all likelihood, he kept a firearm, so Garrick whipped the spoke sideways, thumping it into the shoulder of the saloon-keeper, slamming him against a wall, and he slid to the floor, groaning. Ryder ought to have been reduced by severe pain, but with a great effort he now stepped and swung a blow with his right fist. Garrick ducked under it, avoiding the bunched knuckles, but because of restricted space, could not avoid the heavy forearm and it caught him and hammered him down and to one side and the wagon-spoke fell from his grasp, clattering to the floor. As soon as Ryder saw that happen he closed in, bellowing, and Garrick, up on hands and knees now, went prone on the floor, lashing out with both boots, feeling the jolt right up through his frame as the kick found Ryder and again sent him back.

Coming up, Garrick made a grab for the wagon-spoke and managed to seize it, but one of Ryder's boots now swung hard at him and Garrick's left cheek-bone lanced with fire and his vision blurred as he was knocked violently sideways. Blindly Garrick swept the spoke upwards in both hands and heard the clumping sound it made as it connected somewhere with Ryder's body; but Garrick was trying to clear his vision, trying to get by, even as another savage blow slammed into his ribs and another seemed to burst his lower lip. Yet somehow he managed to reach the open doorway, vaguely hearing Hesse's voice yelling again. In the doorway itself, as he was almost through, he felt himself grasped by the back of the shirt and jerked backwards, buttons flying and the sound of cloth tearing. Instead of trying to wrench free, he went back with the strong pulling of Ryder and snapped his head back sharply, his own senses reeling as he connected with hard bone. For an instant the grasp on his rended shirt relaxed, and he tore himself free, head turning as he arrived in the passageway, only to see Ryder, blood over his mouth, coming at him again, and he was jolted by another blow. In desperation now, Garrick swung around and struck out with the heavy spoke, catching Ryder on one knee, driving a yell from him. Retreating, Garrick passed through the doorway into the kitchen, Ryder floundering after him. Garrick again swung the spoke and vari-coloured glass went flying in a bright shower, then he drove the spoke forward, finding Ryder's throat this time, then caught the man across the side of the head and the big fellow was flung through what was left of the glass door as it had swung partly closed again.

Garrick did not wait, and although moving with much difficulty, managed to get himself out into the yard, lights still leaping across his vision, doubting, even as he emerged into the clean air, that he would be able to make it to his own freight yard and expecting at any instant to feel the hammer-blow of a bullet, Hesse having got hold of the gun he had obviously been seeking.

In the event, it did not happen. Afterwards he was unable to recall how he made the journey from Hesse's to his own yard. Vaguely he was aware of Alford hurrying to help him inside, and once there, the lad having almost to prise the wagon-spoke out of Garrick's grasp. Garrick's entire face seemed swollen, his lower lip was split and his whole torso was carrying a deep ache, and somehow — and he could not bring to mind when it happened — he had sustained an injury that had torn not only skin but flesh from the knuckles of his left hand. Perhaps it had been when, in swinging the club, he had swept some of the glass out of the passage door. The remnants of his shirt were hanging below his waist, only one arm more or less intact. But worst of all, his vision seemed still to be impaired.

Alford wanted to stay with him, then wanted to fetch somebody — anybody — to attend Garrick's injuries, but Garrick limply waved him away. 'Leave me be, Lem. I'll rest up a while an' I'll come right.'

With great reluctance Alford did leave him and Garrick stumbled to his own narrow bed and crawled onto it, wondering vaguely if he would ever be able to breathe deeply or to see clearly again.

11

Well into the following day, Garrick was in a good deal of pain. He ate little and it was only with a great deal of difficulty that he managed to wash himself, but he was unable to shave because of his swollen face. He applied salve to his split lower lip and his facial abrasions and yet more salve and a bandage to the badly scoured knuckles of his left hand. Moving slowly, his ribs hurting, he was feeling as though he had been buffeted by a stampede. Lem Alford was going assiduously about his work but from time to time paused when he caught sight of Garrick, clearly anxious to do something to help, yet by now knowing his employer well enough to hold back until such time as he might be asked.

Through all this pain, however, Garrick felt that he had reason to be thankful for one thing at least; his sight seemed to be returning to normal, objects were no longer blurred at the edges and the darting lights that had awaited the closing of his eyelids, no longer appeared.

Blayrock itself had fallen curiously quiet, having returned, after the departure of the posse, to the daily mundanities of long custom, the townsfolk going about their day-to-day affairs, few range men in evidence, but a little speculation here and there concerning Wenlake and his fresh gather of sworn hard-noses and the chances of their hunting Jim Farrer down. Hesse's saloon, too, stood quietly in the heat, few customers there, its rotund proprietor showing himself only occasionally, walking somewhat slowly; and there was no sign at all of Ryder. What had occurred in a back room at that place only a matter of a few hours before, seemed not to be widely known on the outside. For reasons best known to himself, so Garrick thought later, Hesse was choosing to keep it that way.

After sundown, long after Alford had eaten supper and gone his solitary way to the bunkhouse, Garrick, still in some considerable discomfort, tried to get his own thoughts together but found that Emily's face kept intruding. Of course, he wanted to see her again to try to explain matters, yet the apparent finality of her words and her coldness last time they had met, persistently returned, insisting that he must now face the reality of his having lost her. Late at night, still absorbed with all these sombre thoughts, sitting in a wide cane chair with his legs stretched out, trying to achieve a posture which was not continually uncomfortable, his senses suddenly came alive and he remained quite still, listening. Somewhere outside, perhaps within the yard itself, he was sure there had been a sound.

Very slowly he eased forward, silently cursing the creaking of the cane chair under him and stood up stiffly. He moved to the single lamp that was burning and turned it down, then again stood listening. Nothing. The seconds went ticking by. Maybe he had been mistaken. He had in fact begun to relax when there came another sound. This time he was quite sure that someone was out there, and though it might turn out to be only Lem Alford, he sought out in the darkness the wagon-spoke which he knew to be leaning in a corner where the youngster had placed it once he had been able to get it out of Garrick's hand. Garrick took it up, then with his bandaged left hand slowly slid back the bolt of the yard door. He opened the door. There was an immediate flicker of movement in the nearer darkness, then, hushed but urgent, Farrer's voice said:

'Easy Wes . . . ' Garrick expelled a long, soft breath and lowered the wooden spoke as Farrer came quietly up the two steps and Garrick would have quickly drawn him inside but Farrer then hesitated. 'I got a horse that's gone lame. He's not too bad, I fancy, but he's sure in no shape to run. Wenlake an' his

Goddamn' posse come huntin' me out of the hills. Even now I don't know if I've shook 'em off or not.'

Garrick put the wagon-spoke aside. 'Where's the horse? We'll put him out of sight, in the barn.'

The night was quite moonless but clouds were moving constantly, rendering the yard and all the buildings around it sometimes plainly discernible and at others scarcely so. The tired horse was standing, head drooping, not even hitched, where Farrer had left it just inside the main entrance to the freight yard. Talking to it quietly, Farrer, following at Garrick's heels, led it across the yard to the cavernous barn. While they were installing it there they left one of the tall doors open but lit no lamp, working only by the moon's fitful light, and at Garrick's insistence, when they had removed saddle and blanket, bedroll and canteen from Farrer's animal, put it all up on Garrick's own black.

'If they ever find out what you've

done, Wes, you're in big trouble, I had no right to expect it, comin' here.'

'I'm in trouble already,' Garrick told him, and when they had finished readying the black horse, said: 'Coffee. A meal as well. You'll risk stopping here for that?'

Farrer's weary voice said: 'I'll risk it if you will.'

Inside, the door bolted and the lamp turned up again, Farrer was revealed as a man almost shrunken in the face, older-looking, with an unkempt beard and eyes that were raw from lack of sleep. Yet it was Farrer, when he got a look at the state Garrick was in, who was suddenly shocked.

'What the hell . . . ?'

Garrick shrugged. 'Friend Ryder. Finally I put him away with that wagon-spoke, but more through luck than anything else.' He then told Farrer why he had been up at Hesse's at all, and what he had been shown there.

'Dave Dehl,' said Farrer in a flat tone, as though something had been resolved in his mind, and he eased back onto a chair and dropped his hat to the floor, then sat rubbing broad hands up and down his bearded face. 'It kind of comes together now, Dehl bein' short of money; desperate, more like. It ties right in with somethin' I saw a few nights back.' He stared intently at Garrick who was now starting to fix a meal. 'I saw a herd bein' moved, at night.' When Garrick half turned, Farrer nodded. 'Five riders with two-fifty, maybe nearer three hundred head, comin' in off C Star, up onto Salter Flats, but some ways east of the trail to Georgeville, an' into a valley in the Chater foothills.'

'Five riders.'

'Yeah, well, that was all I saw. After they got the herd into the valley I got a long look at it. I'd heard 'em an' seen 'em comin' from afar off. I was up on higher ground an' all I had to do was keep the horse settled an' stay right there, an' they went by near enough below me. Once they were in that valley they just let the herd settle an' then they all got down an' chewed the fat awhile. Then one of 'em rode out, headed more or less for Blayrock. I thought that one looked somethin' like Dave Dehl, but I couldn't be dead certain. I couldn't think why it should be him anyway.'

'It was,' Garrick said. They counted back, calculating how many nights ago that had been, and then Garrick said: 'That sure does tie up, Jim. The morning after that, he came into Blayrock, ready for Wenlake's new posse.'

Farrer said: 'It must've been a good five, six hours after he left that three of the others headed away in the same direction; one stayed behind with the herd. Among the three that left, one was a real tall, skinny feller.'

'Augie Parr,' said Garrick. 'Those three arrived in Blayrock in no great rush, late in the afternoon; Parr, Eardley and Thomas. All of the bastards that have been on your neck ever since, with Wenlake.'

'An' come close enough to stretchin'

it, I can tell you,' said Farrer. Then, shaking his head: 'Bloody Dave Dehl.'

Garrick nodded. 'Just like you said. Pushed hard for money. Hesse climbin' on his back over it, with Ryder to be the next to take a hand, no doubt. In the finish, there's no friends. Maybe Hagan was in it with Dehl, the two of 'em just cutting out a few head at a time, then leaving 'em up in your canyon for Parr an' his boys to come in an' pick up. But you came across some of 'em, an' that's where it went wrong; an' Smith saw riders he shouldn't have seen. You were just unlucky to be spotted by Clayburgh himself, when he had Hagan an' Dave Dehl along. So that particular arrangement of Dave's went sour, although you were right there to stand accused. For Dehl it was bad luck an' good luck all in one.'

'Maybe Dave had already been paid, an' Parr took it back. No beef, no deal.'

'That's about it, I reckon.' Garrick, still moving slowly, fetched the supper to the table, poured steaming coffee.

'Bolt,' he said then. 'Clayburgh's always reckoned Bolt to be mixed up in it, an' Dehl's always pushed that too; but when I was up at Benning Forks I found out, by chance, that Bolt's had a run of luck at cards over past weeks, good luck there, to match Dave's bad luck at Hesse's. That's where Bolt's saloon money was coming from.'

'What's the best move now, Wes? To be honest, I can't take a lot more o' this. But I still don't fancy tryin' to convince George Wenlake of, well, all I've told you.'

'Chances are, his boys wouldn't let you get that far,' Garrick said. 'Somehow, Parr would find an excuse to blow your head off first. No, leave that part to me, Jim. Let me tackle Wenlake. You get yourself right out of Blayrock an' don't let any of those vipers near you. Give me, say, two days. It's my bet that George will be back here before that, mad as a singed hornet because he's missed you again. You just wait, maybe within sight of the Flying F, but don't go to the house. I'll get through to George if I have to call Dave Dehl to do it; then I'll come out looking for you. If something else happens, if I'm wrong an' George doesn't come in or . . . well, if anything else happens, Lem Alford will come instead, so keep a watch for either of us.'

'I don't like the sound of it, Wes. Before you can spit you could get in a whole lot deeper than you are already. Maybe Wenlake just won't listen, no matter what you say. I tell you Wes, it could turn real nasty real fast.'

'I'll take the risk,' Garrick said. 'You were right when you said Wenlake wouldn't want to hear any of it from you. Now I've got this word on Dave Dehl, some of 'em wouldn't just let me run free anyway. No, it's gone too far for that, Jim, an' I knew before I went to Hesse that, right or wrong I could stand to get my head kicked in.' For a moment he considered laying out for Farrer all that had passed between himself and Liz and Emily Wenlake and how George had been the prime mover in all of that, but in the end he chose not to. It would have to wait until later, until minds were calmer, until all of this other sorry business was resolved; if indeed it was to be resolved at all.

While he had been fully occupied with the unexpected arrival of Farrer and dealing with the horse and fixing food, Garrick had managed to thrust aside some of his physical problems, bu now he sat on a chair, shoulders slumped, his breathing obviously laboured.

'Wes, you sure need somebody to take a look at you.' When Garrick shook his head, Farrer went on: 'What about Emily?' Again Garrick shook his head, but he knew he had to give at least part of an explanation.

'George drove a wedge in there. That's all done with.' Farrer's tired, dust-ravaged eyes continued to regard him steadily. 'Go while you still can,' Garrick advised. 'If they take you Jim, there won't be anything I can do for you. It'll be all over before I can reach George's ear. They can't afford to have it any other way. Your only chance now is through me an' Wenlake, an' that's not a great chance either.'

So Farrer rose, though plainly not liking to leave Garrick in his present poor condition, but at the same time acknowledging the cold sense in all that Garrick had said to him. In fewer than five minutes, Farrer, mounted on Garrick's black horse, going at a walk, left the freight yard and headed away out of Blayrock into the enveloping darkness.

Before another five minutes had elapsed, Garrick, back inside, was stretching himself out on his bed, waves of weariness once again overtaking him. Even so, he knew he must try to rise again at first light and even take Lem Alford into his confidence, at least as far as the presence of Farrer's horse was concerned; for the boy would have to tend the horse, treating the leg that the animal was favouring.

No more than a couple of hours later, however, Garrick came fumbling out of sleep. How long the noise had been going on he did not know, but it soon resolved itself into the loud and urgent shouting of men outside, and the room he was in seemed to be flooded with a strange glow. It was several seconds, however, before the reality penetrated his fuddled mind. Fire.

12

It was the bunkhouse that was fiercely afire, a near-blinding light bursting from its cracking windows, and even as Garrick had come stiffly out into the eerily-lit yard, men, some in their night clothes, had come running, shouting, fetching with them the one means to fight such a blaze, hoarsely forming a chain of slopping buckets, scooping water from every trough in Blayrock, filling more buckets at every frantic pump. Fire, no matter where it broke out in towns such as this, presented a massive, terrifying threat to every other structure, roaring through tinder-dry woodwork, always threatening to leap from one sun-warped building to the next; so all of the people who had come blinking from warm sleep now reacted with a certainty and uniformity that was almost military-like and with an urgency bred from other experiences with such sudden fires, so that a call that scarcely needed to be made could nonetheless be heard over and over, above the roaring of the flames: '*Forget the bunkhouse! Save the places nearest to it!*' For indeed the bunkhouse was already well beyond the ability of men with buckets to save it. Now, all the water that could be got was being hurled over the end wall and the long roof of the horse stalls, white steam rising noisily from them as the wetness was almost instantly dried out again by the pulsing heat that was coming from the burning building.

With several willing helpers, Garrick got all of the horses out, wild-eyed, head-tossing animals wanting to pull away in terror, Garrick making sure that he took charge of the lone horse from the barn, Farrer's, and one by one they got them all the way out through the yard's main entrance and along to the big corral behind Faber's livery, Faber himself, in a nightshirt, waving his arms to help guide them in.

Back at the yard again, Garrick, as close to the roaring bunkhouse, with its now exploding windows as he could get, was asking first one, then another: 'Lem Alford . . . Anybody seen Lem?' No one had. After a time they would not even look at Garrick, simply shaking their heads.

The bucket-chains slaved on. Some of the men had pulled an empty wagon further away from the flames. After twenty minutes, about when the roof of the bunkhouse fell in, sending a storm of sparks into the night sky, those men who were continuing to throw water on nearby woodwork began to see that all their herculean efforts were at last to be rewarded; they had succeeded in preventing this fire at least from spreading any further. In about another half-hour, though a few men were still assiduously soaking other walls and roofs, most other firefighters, some with hands resting on their knees and breathing deeply, were in small groups a short distance away, looking at the heap of glowing embers that, a little less than an hour ago had been the freight yard bunkhouse; and they all knew that somewhere under that still-searing mass must lie the body of the yard-boy, Alford.

Garrick moved around each of these groups, having a quiet word, offering his thanks for what had been driven as much by a desperation to preserve their own premises as by any altruistic impulse. The faces in the yard and in the back street beyond, were picked out strangely in the cherry glow of what was Alford's funeral pyre. Now one or two men with freshly-filled buckets unhurriedly began wetting the edges of it, steam billowing noisily. After a little time even that activity ceased and the townspeople of Blayrock began drifting away.

Garrick, the bandage on his left hand now filthy, a scrap of it hanging loose, his skin blackened, his whole body aching and his head throbbing, turned away to find that Emily Wenlake, a thick coat wrapped around her nightdress, was nearby.

'Lem . . . ?'

He made a vague movement with one hand, shook his head. 'No chance, I guess.'

'Oh Wes . . . Wes, that's dreadful . . . '

He was now utterly exhausted. 'Can't do any more here 'til daylight.'

For just a moment it seemed she might say something else, though he knew that, the yard having returned to near-darkness, she would not be able to see the true state of him. She turned and walked away. Garrick took another look at the fading embers and began to move towards the yard-door, then paused for a minute or two, thinking dully about all that had come to pass over the past few hours. Then with leaden steps he began to move on again, but he had barely reached the door before he heard the horses coming, so waited wearily where he was until Wenlake and his posse came creaking and jingling right into the yard, their horses blowing and stepping as they were brought to a halt.

Leaning forward in the saddle, peering at the shape of Garrick, Wenlake said: 'Seen the fire from 'way outside town. From out there it looked bigger'n it was.'

'It was big enough,' Garrick said. He could not distinguish the individual posse-men but thought he could pick out Parr by the long thin length of him.

'Anybody in there?' Wenlake asked.

'The boy, Alford,' said Garrick.

Wenlake, his horse moving under him, glanced towards the embers but said nothing. Then somebody else, Garrick thought it was Dave Dehl's voice, said:

'It's all over. Let's go.' Several horses were hauled back and away and turned around, their riders jogging them back the way they had come in. Wenlake, however, did not go immediately.

'What was it caused your fire?'

'I don't know yet.'

'Likely he was smokin' in his bunk,' said Wenlake.

'Lem never smoked.'

Wenlake sniffed, pushed his hat back and scratched at his scalp. 'Well, somethin' sure started it.'

'Yeah, an' when it's daylight, I'll try to find out what it was.' When Wenlake seemed about to turn the horse around, Garrick asked: 'You'll still be in Blayrock at sun-up?'

'Just,' Wenlake said. 'We'll be headin' away again as soon as I can roust the boys out.'

'Don't leave until I've talked with you.'

'What? Listen Garrick, I won't have no time to stand around here jawin' with you. So you've had a fire. I sure am sorry about young Alford. It's too bad, but there's nothin' I can do about it. We come near to nailin' that bastard Farrer today, an' by God I aim to get that job done, first thing.'

'George, don't leave until I've talked with you.' Garrick's tone was flat, yet there was something about him and the way he had spoken that caused Wenlake to try to see him more clearly in the dimness. Garrick went inside. He heard Wenlake's horse moving away and eventually, after all the frantic activity of the night, an almost eerie silence fell across the yard and across all of the town.

When daylight came and Garrick, still moving slowly, ventured outside, the first thing he became aware of was the smell of charred wood, a smell that was to return to him on occasions far into the future, even when he was a long way from Blayrock, as though wherever he went, he might never be able to rid himself of it. With great deliberation he examined all of his surviving buildings, inside and out.

Within an hour, Foyle, the Blayrock undertaker and a lugubrious man he fetched with him, Sterrit, arrived to recover the body of Lem Alford, Sterrit was carrying a collapsible stretcher made of two hickory poles and a narrow strip of green canvas. Not long after they began sifting through the still-warm ashes, Wenlake, on foot this time came into the yard.

'This sure is a bad business, Garrick.'

Garrick gave Wenlake a look which caused him to lift his head slightly. 'It's somewhat worse than bad,' Garrick said. 'Come with me.' He walked away, obviously not moving freely, his face still swollen and raw, the rough bandage still on his left hand. If Wenlake wanted to ask him how he had got into such a state, he suppressed the temptation, for there was something else about Garrick this morning, and it had nothing to do with his obvious injuries, which had persuaded even Wenlake to step warily. So, silently, he followed Garrick around the faintly-smoking, blackened mess that yesterday had been the bunkhouse, to the farther side of the horse stalls, and there, paused. Although what Garrick was pointing to had been partially trampled and scattered during the frenzied activities of fire-fighting, it was still perfectly clear what it was that had been there; a heap of wood-shavings, some blackened, plainly having been set alight by someone, but which had failed to ignite properly.

Wenlake's face, usually hawkish, often sardonic, now simply looked tired. 'Jesus Christ!' Wenlake said. When Garrick offered no comment whatsoever about what he had just shown the peace officer, Wenlake eventually said: 'Do you have any ideas?'

'A few,' Garrick said, then turned to stare fully at Wenlake. 'But it so happens I don't have proof, an' I for one, don't go off half-cocked, working on what might be so.'

Wenlake flushed, at once aware of the thrust, reverting to his customary sharpness of manner, and started to say: 'Now, you look here, Garrick — '

'No!' Garrick's voice was suddenly a whiplash that made even Wenlake blink. 'My turn George, an' I don't give a spit in hell who you are. Let me tell you something, an' you can do whatever you like about it. One of the horses that we got out of this yard an' that we took along to Faber's, belongs to Jim Farrer. You can go look at the brand for yourself. Right now, Farrer's got my black under him an' I hope it gets him well away from you an' your hired scum, even clear out of this territory.' Before Wenlake could come bursting angrily in again, Garrick told him in a cold, hard tone, about Dave Dehl and Hesse, about Augie Parr and what kind of bastard he happened to be, and about the maybe three hundred head of C Star beef even now spirited away into a valley below the Chaters, and said then: 'My pick is that Dehl's been paid off by now an' in the next couple of days most of your damn' posse is all set to melt away an' you'll never see a whisker of any of 'em again. You'll be left to look the fool. It's likely they've worked this seam out, so they'll move on somewhere else, find another Dave Dehl. God knows there's plenty of 'em around.' When a voice called and they went back into the yard they found that Foyle and Sterrit had got the pitiful, charred remains of the boy, Alford, onto the stretcher. Garrick looked at a subdued Wenlake. 'An' I'll tell you this for nothing, George; I'll find out who it was that did this, an' when I do, don't you bother about swamping out your cage, ready, for there'll be nothing left worth turning the key on.'

Now Wenlake did manage to find his voice but this time there was no bluster in it. 'Now, you wait, Wes. If it is like you say it is, an' from what you've said, my bet for this fire would have to be Ryder. But whoever it was, it's my job to go askin' the questions, an' it's my job to front Dave Dehl an' anybody else that's in it with him, not yours. Mine.'

Somewhat grudgingly, bitter though he was, Garrick had to acknowledge that for all his pomposity, the man had some sand, for he would be perfectly aware of what he would be up against. But Garrick said:

'I think you're a damn' fool, George.

If it goes real sour you could take one of 'em, maybe even two, but after that you won't stand a Goddamn' chance.'

'Notwithstandin',' said Wenlake doggedly, 'as the law here it's *my* chance to take, whatever that might be. That's what I take the county's money for. Anyway, by the looks of things, you're in no shape to front anybody. Who was it did that to you?'

'Ryder.' Wenlake nodded, then they both stood looking sombrely on as Foyle and Sterrit carried their pitifully-laden green stretcher out of the yard. Of Alford, Garrick suddenly said: 'I don't even know where he was from, or if he had a family somewhere.' And in a lower voice: 'I could've sent him out with Steve Elder, an' didn't.' After that there seemed nothing more to add.

Presently Wenlake said: 'Right now I'm goin' back on down to the office an' clear up a couple of things there, an' then I'm goin' up to Hesse's where Dave will no doubt be, an' have this out with him face to face.'

Garrick shrugged. 'It's your hide.'

'They won't dare buck the elected law,' Wenlake said. 'They won't be that stupid. Anyway, I want to try to get Dave out of there on his own if I can, for a start.'

'I don't think they're stupid either,' said Garrick, 'but these are the kind of roosters, if they sniff which way the new wind's blowing, won't give you a clear chance.' It occurred to Garrick then, however, that George Wenlake really did believe that the law, as he saw it, even in a town such as Blayrock, still carried with it an inviolable authority, even among such hard men as Parr and Eardley and Thomas. Therefore it was with mixed feelings that he watched Wenlake go striding away.

A short time after that, curious to find out what was happening, Garrick went out of the yard and along the narrow street to where it joined Main. A number of people were about, moving along the boardwalks, all apparently going about their normal business, though he could see nothing of Wenlake; but there was a single mare harnessed to a buckboard at the hitching rail outside Wenlake's office. Garrick glanced again in the opposite direction and it was then that he saw the peace officer who, having apparently been elsewhere for some reason, was now in the act of crossing Main diagonally, towards Hesse's, outside of which establishment several horses were hitched. Garrick waited a moment or two then moved slowly and still painfully along the boardwalk, keeping his attention on the place into which Wenlake had now disappeared. He had no way of knowing what transpired once the peace officer got inside Hesse's, but whatever it was, it produced an early result, for Dave Dehl came out onto the boardwalk up there and right behind him was George Wenlake, walking in what seemed to be an easy manner, hands empty and swinging freely. Maybe he had merely said that he wanted to speak to Dehl privately, for there appeared to be no sense of tension as far as Garrick could judge at that distance.

When they were some hundred feet away from Hesse's, however, Dehl stopped and turned and it was then that an argument apparently broke out, for Wenlake also halted and appeared to be telling Dehl to keep walking. Not only that, but three other men had come out of Hesse's and were observing Dehl and Wenlake; Parr, Eardley and Thomas. Garrick now kept his attention on those three, quite uneasy that Wenlake, his back to them, would be unaware that they had come out. Dave Dehl though, who would have been able to see them, glanced then at a nearby alley and went lunging for it, even as Garrick, not knowing whether it would do any good or not, bellowed: 'Behind you, George!'

Wenlake did get his head partly around but by that time Eardley was clearing a long pistol away and by the time Wenlake realized that the unbelievable was actually happening, there was the startlingly loud sound of the pistol going off and a wash of powder smoke around the distant Eardley, and Wenlake, punched hard, was down and rolling on the boardwalk, and a lot of people were getting the hell out of the way. Dehl had not reappeared and Garrick assumed that the C Star foreman had continued running along the alley.

Wenlake had gone down outside the general store and from there a man wearing a white apron appeared, only to retreat when he looked to his left and saw Eardley with the heavy pistol still in his hand, ready to fire again. Garrick, though realizing equally that to approach the fallen Wenlake might be suicidal, began to go towards him at a half jog, and though he was hurting at every step.

13

Garrick was not quite managing to run, but as he drew nearer to the fallen man, saw that Wenlake was now doing his utmost to crawl away, his upper body and his arms apparently functioning but one of his legs — his left one — dragging as though it had had a considerable weight attached to it, and there was rich blood all over his pants. Still Garrick came on, though well aware of all his own hurts, feeling dangerously exposed, too, knowing that the dangerous group still standing up by Hesse's had now seen him; and he was concerned that he had no notion of where Dehl might have got to. For all Garrick knew, the C Star foreman might suddenly reappear behind him, and thus he might well find himself trapped between Dehl and the other armed men.

Wenlake's eyes were glazed with pain and he had left behind him a blood mark dragged along the boardwalk. As Garrick stooped to him, somebody yelled something and almost immediately there came another loud gunshot and dust jumped sharply in the street near the edge of the boardwalk. Garrick managed to get hold of Wenlake's left arm and contrived to put it across his own shoulders, to hold it at the wrist with his own bandaged hand, then drained though he was by his own injuries, using his considerable strength, slowly straightened up, drawing the groaning Wenlake with him, and then got his right arm hooked around the peace officer's middle. 'Come on George, for Chrissake, before they blow our asses off!' There was some response from Wenlake, whose breath was gasping out harshly as a result of his pain, but Garrick found that he had to do most of the work as they began to go ever so slowly and unsteadily along the boardwalk.

Now there came more gunfire and dust jumped again and lead slammed into woodwork and Garrick, with his heavily-dragging companion, bumping along as close as was possible to a shopfront, came to the mouth of an alleyway and with an immense effort managed to get Wenlake down off the boardwalk and around the corner even as further gunfire boomed and lead came humming at them. Yet those who were up in front of Hesse's had shown no inclination whatsoever to give chase and Garrick could only conclude that, having downed Wenlake, hitting him solidly, they were not at all concerned that Garrick nor, for that matter anybody else in Blayrock, could be in a position to pose any kind of threat to them. It was a kind of arrogance.

How he got George Wenlake all the way along the hot, fly-darting alley without both of them collapsing, and then, in another agonizingly slow journey, around into the yard behind the Blayrock jail, Garrick could not afterwards remember clearly. What he did become aware of as he staggered in there was that Emily, holding her skirts up, had come running out, her face pale and her eyes wide in alarm, and that, incomprehensibly, Liz Farrer had followed her out.

Somehow, together, they managed to get the wounded man, who obviously had taken a bullet in the back of the left thigh, a bullet that had made an ugly wound, perhaps partially flattening on impact, inside the house where eventually they placed him face down on his bed, unmindful of the blood which now seemed to be everywhere. Garrick himself, relieved of his burden, head hanging, resting against a wall, chest heaving, his shirt sodden with sweat, vaguely waved away all concerns except those for Wenlake, and after a few minutes, without any further talk, and though somewhat unsteady on his feet, simply walked back outside. He did not even look over his shoulder but continued on, his mind now made up on his next course, and presently came again into his own yard.

Inside, he took the shotgun down from its pegs, and from the cupboard, fetched the box of cartridges with their waxy red bodies and shining end-caps and put them on the table. He then selected fifteen, examining each with great care for possible distortion. From a peg behind the door he took down a denim jacket with two capacious pockets and, sweating though he was, put it on and fastened the five front studs. In either pocket he placed five cartridges; the other five he loaded into the shotgun, four of them into the tubular magazine below the barrel. Then, dropping his hat onto a chair, he poured water from a pitcher into a large enamel bowl and sluiced his stubbly face and hair. His face was still swollen and there was a dull ache in his head, and any sudden or laborious movement that he made was still stiffly painful to him. Nevertheless, his hat on again, he took up the shotgun. An awkward weapon, its levering mechanism not particularly quick to operate, its uncompromising potential to damage the shoulder of any unskilled shooter who was unwary of its mulish kick, in experienced hands and at close quarters it was truly a fearsome thing. Yet clumsy as this gun might be considered to be, Garrick himself had manifold reservations about the effectiveness of the large and heavy .44 calibre pistols that were so commonly in use, in the hands of all but the unusually skilled. He was well aware, however, that during perhaps the next half-hour, he might get himself into a situation from which he could not possibly come out alive, not only because of his poor physical shape, but because there were very dangerous men who were now in Blayrock, and who, in the shooting down of George Wenlake, had demonstrated their utter contempt for the elected law in a way that most of the citizens would once have thought scarcely possible. Indeed, George Wenlake had spoken as though he believed himself to be fireproof. But Garrick was now consumed by a deep-reaching anger. He was not by any means a fighting man, for though physically strong he was unschooled in violence in the way that Parr and his associates clearly were; but too many events had now accumulated for him to stand aside, dire acts against the Farrers, against himself and sadly, by association, against the boy, Lem Alford, whose life was now ended because of that; and against Wenlake too, poor, fussy, pompous yet undeniably brave Wenlake; and the other serious personal damage arising from it all had been that which had come about between himself and Emily. Now, he felt, nothing would be the same again.

But the odds against him were huge. Garrick felt that, to begin with, he had to have some small piece of luck, and when finally he came to the corner of a sidestreet not far from Hesse's, and risked a look, he saw that he had been at least granted that much. Not only had the shooters now vanished, presumably back into the saloon, but their horses, ears flicking, tails switching, were all still hitched to the rail outside. Garrick took a deep breath. To ponder too long over this would be to not do it at all, so under the curious stares of the few people who had now ventured back onto Main, he went forward, carrying his shotgun, and as quickly as he was able, directly to the horses, and one by one, concentrating on the task and not even looking towards the saloon, he unhitched the animals.

Sensing that something else unpleasant was soon about to happen, the people on Main who had been watching him now began seeking cover again. The horses, though freed, seemed disinclined to move away so Garrick backed off about ten paces, put the hard rubber butt-plate of the shotgun to his shoulder, aimed it upwards at an angle of about forty-five degress and let go a booming blast. That sure moved the horses. Two of them first rearing, they all went scattering, the reins flying. Garrick was retreating also, and stepped around into a narrow alley, levering a fresh load in, ejecting the spent cartridge from the slot in the left side of the gun.

Now there was some activity at Hesse's, for though Garrick drew carefully back, showing as little of himself as possible, he saw Parr, then Eardley, then Thomas emerge, and then Dave Dehl who evidently, upon running from Wenlake, had gone right around and in the back door. Then came the big figure of Ryder, limping and with his head bandaged. There was some arm waving when they realized that the horses had been far and widely scattered. Thomas had a pistol drawn but could see nothing to shoot at. For the second time on this day, Blayrock had taken on an unreal stillness.

Dehl said something and then Parr, in a deep, carrying voice said: 'It was likely that bastard Garrick. Before we pull out we'll comb this dump for him an' teach him it was a bad mistake to go shovin' his oar in.' Then, quieter: 'Buck, see if you can round up the damn' horses.'

Hesse had also put in an appearance, standing in the doorway, holding the batwings open. 'Watch out for that damn' shotgun of his. He's reckoned to be some handler of it.'

Garrick had managed to catch most of what Parr had said and thought that, in one sense, their spreading out might offer him a better chance at individuals, yet in another would present him with what would be a nerve-racking stalk through Blayrock, never knowing what the next corner might bring to him. So before retreating further, he watched them disperse.

★ ★ ★

With his precise, cat-like steps, Eardley came along a back street that paralleled Main, Eardley of the neat but sombre-hued clothing, his black leather vest fully buttoned, his very widebrimmed hat set squarely on his head, leather thongs hanging loose on either side of his face. Calm, unhurried, his fish-like eyes taking in everything, all visible windows, all the untidy back-lots, a cigar clenched between his widely-spaced teeth, the large, carefully-oiled pistol in his hand but hanging by his side. Cigar smoke faintly trailed him as he walked. Parr, as they parted, had emphasized haste in getting this over and done with, but as his careful nature dictated, Eardley would take his own time and do his part in it in his own way, especially as he was now regretting his uncharacteristically casual attitude in the earlier shooting at Garrick and Wenlake. He was very good with the long pistol, Eardley, and backed himself to blow Garrick down with it at a distance greater than that which he personally believed to be the effective range of any shotgun, no matter who was holding it.

Any yard that he came to Eardley

entered and kicked open the sun-warped doors of outbuildings; and he crossed the narrow, rutted street to examine the musty interior of a barn, then came back, lifted his expressionless eyes when a woman looked out from a back doorway, moved on, approached the rear of a café where there were several open sacks of fly-infested garbage, the stench of which Eardley's cigar could not even hope to defeat. Eardley half averted his face, almost gagging at the foulness of the smell; so having approached to within ten feet of it he turned and walked away; but at the very last moment he was aware that a man had stood up from right in among the putrid sacks, a tall man wearing denim pants, a studded denim jacket with bulging pockets, a shallow-crowned, battered grey hat, a man with a badly swollen, stubbly face and one bandaged hand and holding a shotgun the muzzle of which was about three quarters of an inch in diameter, but to Eardley, looked a whole lot larger than that.

Eardley, however, did well. Instead of turning with his feline speed, reversing the direction in which he had been going, he continued a complete turn to the right, at the same time swinging the pistol-arm up, even though the move meant that he had to take his eyes off the shotgunner for the space of time that it took him to make the full turn. Even so, fast though it was, it was not fast enough. The thumping explosion of the shotgun was stunning, smoke bursting forth, and the still-fisted shot hit Eardley squarely on the right side beneath his lifting arm and hurled him to the rough ground, his life's blood flying from him, and even as he went down, the pistol he was still holding discharged, but into the air. By the time Eardley stopped his twitching movements and the myriad flies descended on him, Garrick, working the stiff lever beneath the shotgun, ejecting the spent, smoking cartridge case, bringing a fresh one into the chamber, was already on the move himself, going out of the yard at an awkward, pain-racked jog, knowing that it would not be long before others arrived.

Buck Thomas, having at this time recovered only one of the horses and hitched it outside Hesse's, was on his way to get hold of another when he heard the heavy and unmistakable thump of the shotgun and also what sounded like a .44 going off. Further along Main, Parr reappeared from a side-street to look, then shrugging his narrow shoulders, called:

'See anything?'

Thomas shook his head, now abandoning his plans to recover the second horse, drew his pistol and at once prepared to head away towards where the sounds of shooting seemed to have come from. Parr made a slow, circling motion with one of his hands, indicating that he also would go, but not directly. Thomas nodded, went jogging off, having made up his mind to go right on through Hesse's, coming out in the yard and, beyond that, onto a back street. Also at a loping jog, the long-limbed Parr angled away towards an alley that would lead him onto that same street. Both of them had passed from sight when first Dave Dehl, then the limping and bandaged Ryder, came out on Main but on the opposite side. Dehl, gun in hand, crossed Main and cautiously followed the route that Parr had taken, though he did not know that at the time. Ryder, an old pistol belonging to Hesse in his hand, stood watching him go. Clearly Ryder did not know what to do, so wandered vaguely towards Hesse's on the opposite side of the street. However, on his way there he glanced back along Main and stopped short, blinking, looking down the length of that street, for he could have sworn that he had caught a glimpse of Garrick, also slipping across but going the opposite way, going in among buildings in an area that Ryder had recently quit. Ryder blinked again. Since he had been injured by Garrick's wagon-spoke his right eye had been almost closed, so he could not be quite certain who it was he had seen. Nonetheless, believing that he should go and find out, rather than raising an alarm needlessly and perhaps end up looking foolish, he went trudging back the way he had come.

Ryder spent several minutes, looking, walking around buildings and yards, sometimes calling out to people whom he became aware were watching him go by. 'Yuh seen the freight man? Seen Garrick?' Sometimes there was a quick shake of the head while at others there was only a withdrawal from door or window. A lot of people in Blayrock were afraid of the big man from Hesse's. After a while Ryder grew tired of looking around to no result, and put the old pistol, with which he had felt neither familiar nor comfortable, down inside his wide leather belt. Only a moment or two after that, coming around the side of a barn, he saw Garrick who, at the same instant, saw Ryder. Any of the people who were able to observe what was going on saw Garrick who, while he knew that the range was too great to be effective, let go a shot at Ryder, who was trying to tug the pistol free of his belt, and went diving to the ground as a wide pattern of lead shot spattered the wall of the barn, some of it stinging him sharply, even breaking the skin. He got up onto his knees, working at the butt of the big pistol, knowing that Garrick, perhaps seeing his difficulty, was now running in on him, closing the range so that if he did not clear the pistol away now, he was in real trouble. Suddenly it came free and Ryder extended a long arm and fired, the booming shot washing gunsmoke back on him, the pistol kicking upward; but Garrick was still coming on unchecked, and then, as Ryder was lining up for another crack at him, incredibly, stopped in his tracks, the shotgun up, and if Ryder heard the thumping explosion of it, then it was the last sound he did hear on earth, for the charge, heavily bunched this time, flung him savagely back against the wall of the barn and by the time Garrick walked up to him, levering in another cartridge — the last one in the gun — Ryder, the pistol gone from his hand, was still sliding against the wall, leaving a red smear behind him to lie quivering, but already dead, in the hot sun. Garrick's sweat-slick face was a mask, his eyes narrowed, showing no evidence of pity, recalling the awful charred thing that had been taken from the burned-down bunkhouse and put onto the canvas stretcher. Garrick turned away but was still moving slowly. The effort it had demanded of his beaten body to get in close to Ryder for an effective shot had taken its toll; but he had taken the unexpected Ryder out, and by good luck and some cunning, the dangerous Eardley as well. Maybe, on his own, that was the best he could hope for, lacking the deadly skills of Parr, for one, and in all probability those of Thomas. Garrick thought that, in his present condition, he had probably done better than he had any right to hope, and there was

Dave Dehl too, still with them. Garrick had the feeling that those three would now begin to call all of the shots and that the best thing he could do now would be to go to ground and try to wait them out.

While Dave Dehl had still been on his way towards the sounds of earlier gunfire, Parr and Thomas were already on their way back, not having wanted to spend any more time than was absolutely necessary around the back of the café, and met him.

'Where's Eard?'

'Dead,' Thomas said. 'Bastard blew half of his chest away. Bastard shotgunner.'

'By God,' said Parr, 'he ain't about to get in close enough to me to get it done.' Parr was deeply angry. 'Before I quit this fly-blown dump I'm gonna kick the shit out o' this rooster, no mistake.'

It was then that they heard, somewhere beyond the opposite side of Main, the solid thud of the shotgun, then a heavy calibre pistol and quite soon after that, another shotgun blast. They broke into a run, all three, pistols drawn.

Not long afterwards they found Ryder, much as earlier, they had found Eardley.

'Christ!' Dehl said, repelled by the sight, the shattered body, the copious blood and already, the moving mass of flies. Dehl was becoming edgy now, very anxious that this Garrick should be nailed. It was Garrick, after all, who had pressured Hesse in the first place, the shrewd bastard, and incredibly, having fought with Ryder, had lived to walk away; and now here was Ryder, broken, dead at Garrick's hands. Yes, Dehl badly wanted Garrick put away. Equally he wanted to get right out of the Godforsaken place and move on in company with Parr and Thomas, for there was no doubt whatsoever that there could be no going back to Clayburgh's ranch. He would deal with Garrick, and then he was finished in this stretch of country.

'I'll find this bastard,' Parr said, 'if I have to kick in every door there is in this cesspool.'

It was then that Dehl thought of something. 'That Wenlake woman. If we can't find Garrick, mebbe he could be persuaded to come to us.'

Thomas grinned and snapped his fingers. 'By God, a woman. That's it.'

'As long as we can get it done without any more pissin' around,' Parr said. 'I now want to get shut o' this dump.'

By now Garrick was well away from the place where Ryder lay; but if people had been reluctant to get anywhere near Ryder when he had been pacing around, there was an almost equal reluctance to be seen to be helping Garrick. He could understand it. To be in his proximity was to risk being a target, and he was after all only a freighter, up against men who had not hesitated to shoot Wenlake himself. A little more time was to elapse before there was anything like a wide awareness that two of these men already lay dead at Garrick's hands. Garrick now wondered when he might expect to see Steve Elder back in Blayrock; not that he had any design to draw him into this. It had been none of his affair. And now, Parr, Thomas and Dehl could be expected to increase their efforts to flush Garrick out, and if they should somehow manage to corner him he knew that he would be no match for them. Presumably, however, they were continuing to carry only pistols and he could not recall whether or not there had been rifles on any of their horses; but he thought there had to be at least one rifle among them. He could not have known it but even as this thought came to him, Thomas was saying to Parr: 'What about a rifle? I should go down an' find the other horses an' get rifles. That way we might not have to get close enough so he can use the damn' shotgun.'

Parr thought about it, then shook his head positively. 'Can't wait that long. He won't have the sand to get in close to all three of us. No, we'll go pay a call on

216

Wenlake an' set up the bait. After that, I reckon it won't take long.'

Thomas nodded, accepting it, but sweating as he was, peeled off the calfskin jacket that he had been wearing and slung it over one shoulder. His leathery face was beaded with sweat and the whitish scar across his jaw seemed more that usually visible.

When Dave Dehl, Augie Parr and Buck Thomas came out on Main about half way along, Garrick saw them and wondered what the hell was in the wind now. From cover, behind piled-up casks, Garrick watched as, walking with drawn pistols, they angled across the street, and he could soon see that if they continued along the same line then they must surely arrive outside the Blayrock jail where the placid mare with the buckboard still stood; Liz Farrer's. Garrick retreated down an alley, suddenly apprehensive about Parr's intentions, and if he had read them right, desperate to get between these men and Liz and the Wenlakes.

The now extended pause since the last burst of gunfire had again brought faces to windows, the bolder hearts into open doorways. Emily Wenlake, almost gaunt from anxiety, had glanced countless times from her own windows, perhaps hoping virtually against hope for someone to appear and tell her that the gunmen had ridden away. Wenlake, lying on his bed, his face lined with pain, having undergone the removal of lead from his thigh, and though he was now heavily bandaged, the leg still throbbed and his body was slick with sweat. He had had the presence of mind, however, to have Emily close and bolt the door of the office that gave onto Main; and left alone, had reached above his head to pull the heavy pistol out of the hanging holster. But after doing that he had felt exhausted and was bathed in new sweat.

Wenlake had realized that Liz Farrer's purpose in coming here at all had been to talk with Emily about Garrick, and she had indeed come determinedly, no matter what Wenlake himself might have thought about it; but other events had swiftly overtaken whatever had passed between the women, and when necessity demanded it, they had simply worked together as best they had been able, to remove the big slug and clean and treat the ugly wound that Wenlake had. His thoughts were confused, his personal recriminations no doubt yet to come, perhaps in the still night hours, and only when this affair was all done with. Cursing his own impotence, he would have given a lot to know what the hell was going on out there and whether Wes Garrick was alive or dead. There had been several thumping reports from a shotgun and the sounds of heavy .44s going off as well, but now an almost eerie quiet had fallen once again. Then he heard Liz Farrer saying: 'It's Wes.'

Indeed, Garrick was in the yard, shotgun in one hand and waving the other sharply, and the message was unmistakable: '*Get down! They're coming!*' Just as quickly as he had appeared, he slipped away among the outbuildings. The brief glance they had had of him, however, had shown him to be about at the end of his tether, and it had clearly been Emily's immediate impulse to go out to him, but Liz had taken her arm with firm fingers.

'It can't do any good.'

They bolted the back door, and Wenlake, his voice faint, asked: 'What is it? What's up?' When Emily came to his door and told him, he said: 'Christ!' He took up the pistol but at once had to rest it down again; but he said urgently: 'Both of you, go get down on the floor of the cage.'

'Pa — !'

'Go! Now!' Even the effort of raising his voice sent a wave of nausea through him, yet he was satisfied when he heard Emily say to Liz:

'Come on. It makes good sense to go in there.'

Suddenly the back door was rapped sharply and the latch was rattled. Parr's voice then called: 'Wenlake! If yuh can't open this, tell the woman to do it!' When there was no response. 'Ten seconds, that's all!'

Sweat coursing down his face, shirt sticking to him, his left trouser leg fallen open where they had cut it to get at the wound, Wenlake summoned into his arms the strength of fear and hauled himself sideways, dropping the pistol to the bedside mat, then, fiery agony shooting through his thigh, rolled right over; then almost crying out with pain, he slid down and, bracing his hands on the floor, half fell from the bed. Fireworks behind his tightly-shut eye-lids were almost bright enough to dazzle him, but with one further effort born of desperation and by pushing the heavy pistol across the floor in front of him, he managed to get as far as the open doorway, through which, at an angle, he could see the yard door, and even as he did so, Parr's voice said: 'That's it, then.' Two loud explosions followed and holes were punched in the door near the latch, long, clean-looking slivers of wood spitting away. Boots began kicking at the door. Lying propped on his elbows, the long pistol now grasped in both his hands, his vision swimming, Wenlake shot once . . . twice, the door again shivering with the impact of lead, and there erupted from outside a scream of agony.

'Oh, Jesus . . . Oh shit Augie . . . ' There was a lot more shouting that was unintelligible to Wenlake, his eyes squeezed shut again, sweating profusely, the smoking pistol suddenly unbearably heavy, resting on the floor. Then again a raised voice from outside, but sounding slightly further off:

'Shotgunner!' And on the heels of that, the heavy thump of the gun.

Garrick, from the moment that Parr and the others had come into the yard, and from where he stood just behind one of the outbuildings, had been able to see them approaching the yard door. Having had but one cartridge of his first five remaining in the gun he had also taken the opportunity to refill the magazine with four fresh loads. Even so, he recognized that he could well be confronted with all three of them firing at him, and the shotgun's lever action was not fast to operate, and he could easily be badly exposed while reloading. He had heard them calling out, and when a man let go with a .44 at the yard door, prayed that Emily and Liz were well out of the way. Then gunfire sounded from inside the house and Thomas, letting fall his pistol, screamed and went spinning away, the jacket that had been draped over his shoulders, falling also. It seemed that he had been hit both in the knee and in the chest, and was in agony, rolling in the dusty yard, almost halfway to where Garrick was. Parr and Dave Dehl had gone backing away from the dangerous door and when Dehl came to Thomas to see how bad he was, Garrick, the butt-plate to his shoulder, stepped clear of the outbuilding. Dehl did his best to swing his pistol up to bear on him, at the same time shouting a warning: 'Shotgunner!'

But Garrick stood his ground and in a blast of fire and a wash of blue smoke, shot him, the fist-bunched charge hitting him with a distinct, wet-sounding, solid slap, punching him hard backwards, to go sliding on his shoulders in the yard.

Parr, in a fury, had turned and fired, only to find that his target had gone down amid dust and smoke, full length, half rolling to one side, levering the shotgun, and though seeming to take a long time to reload, blasting again even as Parr had retreated; but spreading shot struck Parr, starting bright blood from him in a score of places. Parr fired, the long pistol bucking in his hand, but missed, seeing only a bloodied haze through the fires in his eye sockets and perhaps, as Eardley might have done, heard the next thump of the shotgun only as he passed through the portals of hell. Thomas had stopped screaming and lay quite still.

When, eventually, Emily slid the bolt back and opened the riven door,

Garrick, having set his shotgun aside, was already on the steps, gently pushing her back inside. 'The yard's not a good place to be. There's nothing to be done for any of 'em. I'll go get Foyle to take 'em out.' Her fingers touching her lips, her face ashen, she did not answer. Garrick went inside and helped get George Wenlake back onto his bed, the peace officer now near to losing consciousness. But Garrick said: 'You stopped Buck Thomas for good an' all, George, an' it made the difference.' He could not be certain that Wenlake had even heard him. Garrick went out through the kitchen to find that a pale and shaken Liz Farrer had followed him.

'Wes . . . Wes, I've talked with Emily. I think she believes what I've said to her. It should be all right now.'

Garrick, weary beyond belief, nodded. 'We'll see Liz. We'll see.' He went outside, picked up the shotgun, broke it open and with the stock grasped in one hand at the front of him, the barrel angled over his shoulder and down his back, walked away. On his way along Main to seek out Foyle, he glanced down the sidestreet where his freight yard was and saw the wagon with Elder on it, about to turn in through the gates. Garrick waved him to a halt and as he drew nearer, Elder said; 'Wes, the bunkhouse . . . what the hell?'

'All in good time,' said Garrick. Then: 'Don't look for Lem. He's not there. When I can, I'll tell you.' He went walking back the way he had come. He was uncertain just how much time had elapsed since he had seen George Wenlake angling across Main towards Hesse's on his way to talk with Dave Dehl, but it seemed to be a very long time. It seemed a longer time, too, since he and Emily had sat together, talking warmly of what their plans and aims were. '*I think she believes what I've said to her. It should be all right now.*' Was that what Liz had said? On Main again he glanced towards the Blayrock jail. The buckboard had gone. She would be heading out again to try to find her husband, to end the nightmare, perhaps for both of them. Garrick walked on, his whole body aching, his face and head throbbing, towards the parlour where Foyle would be, so he could tell him where the dead men lay.

THE END

GUNS OF THE GAMBLER

M. Duggan

Destitute gambler Ben Crow arrives in Mallory keen to claim his inheritance, only to discover that rancher Edward Bacon has other ideas. Set up by Miss Dorothy, who had fooled him completely, Ben finds himself dangling on the end of a rope. Saved from death, Ben sets off in pursuit of Miss Dorothy, determined upon retribution. However, his quest for vengeance turns into a rescue mission when she is kidnapped by a crazy man-burning bandit.

SIDEWINDER

John Dyson

All Flynn wants is to be Marshal of Tucson, but he is framed by the territory's richest rancher, Frank Buchanan, and thrown into Yuma prison. Five years later Flynn comes out, intent on clearing his name and burning for vengeance. Fists thud, knives flash and bullets fly as he rides both sides of the law and participates in kidnapping and double-dealing. He is once again arrested for a murder of which he is innocent. Can he escape the noose a second time?

THE BLOODING OF JETHRO

Frank Fields

When Jethro Smith's family is murdered by outlaws, vengeance is the one thing on his mind. He meets the brother of one of the murderers, who attempts to exploit Jethro's grudge in the pursuit of his own vendetta. The local preacher, formerly a sheriff, teaches Jethro how to use a gun. With his new-found skills, Jethro and his somewhat unwelcome friend pit themselves against seemingly impossible odds. Whatever the outcome lead would surely fly.

SEVEN HELLS AND A SIXGUN

Jack Greer

Jim Cayman had been warned about Daphne Rankin, his boss's wife, and her little ways. When Daphne made a play for Jim and he resisted, the result was painful and about what he had feared. But suddenly matters went beyond the expected and he found himself left to die an awful death. Only then did he realise that there was far more than a woman scorned. He vowed that if he could escape from the hell-hole he would surely solve the mystery — and settle some scores.

CRISIS IN CASTELLO COUNTY

D. A. Horncastle

The first thing Texas Ranger Sergeant Brad Saunders finds when he responds to an urgent call for help from the local sheriff is the corpse of the public prosecutor floating in the Nueces River. Soon Brad finds himself caught in the midst of a power struggle between a gang of tough western outlaws and a bunch of Italian gangsters, whose thirst for bloody revenge knows no bounds. Brad was going to have all his work cut out to end the bloody warfare — and stay alive!